## "Maybe I do need you. Would that be so bad?"

Wiley turned. "Macy, that wouldn't just be bad, but a full-on disaster. I thought we'd already been over this?"

"You know what I think?" She passed on his right, giving him too good a view of her amazing behind.

"No, and I don't care."

"I think you're chicken."

He snorted. "I think if you don't stop walking backward, you're gonna fall."

"You'll catch me."

"Nope."

Sure enough, she tripped. Though his reflexes were sluggish on the meds, his hands connected with her waist in time to pull her up against him.

"You're welcome," he said with his mouth an inch from hers.

"Told you you'd catch me." Her smile brought on a heat wave that had nothing to do with the day's waning sun. "Wiley James, I think there's a part of you, who, to this very day, still wonders what might've happened had my dad not interrupted."

Dear Reader,

I've written over thirty books for Harlequin American Romance, and I've never had a story affect me so deeply. Without giving away too much of Wiley and Macy's journey, let's just say a lot of their issues center around this SEAL's heartbreaking PTSD (post-traumatic stress disorder).

One of the things that most surprised me about this anxiety disorder is that it's not strictly a military issue. According to ptsdunited.org, "PTSD affects about 7.7 million American adults in a given year, though the disorder can develop at any age, including childhood." Most sufferers have been exposed to not only combat, but "...terrorist attacks, natural disasters, serious accidents, assault or abuse, or even sudden and major emotional losses."

"An estimated 8% of Americans—24.4 million people have PTSD at any given time. That is equal to the total population of Texas." Also surprising to me is the fact that, "One out of every nine women develops PTSD, making them about twice as likely as men."

If you or a loved one suffers from this often silent and misunderstood struggle, please know there are many organizations ready to help. Your primary care physician or ptsdunited.org is a great place to begin the healing journey.

All my best,

*Laura Marie*

# THE BABY
# AND THE
# COWBOY SEAL

———

## LAURA MARIE ALTOM

HARLEQUIN® AMERICAN ROMANCE®

Recycling programs
for this product may
not exist in your area.

ISBN-13: 978-0-373-75603-2

The Baby and the Cowboy SEAL

Copyright © 2016 by Laura Marie Altom

All rights reserved. Except for use in any review, the reproduction or utilization of this work in whole or in part in any form by any electronic, mechanical or other means, now known or hereinafter invented, including xerography, photocopying and recording, or in any information storage or retrieval system, is forbidden without the written permission of the publisher, Harlequin Enterprises Limited, 225 Duncan Mill Road, Don Mills, Ontario M3B 3K9, Canada.

This is a work of fiction. Names, characters, places and incidents are either the product of the author's imagination or are used fictitiously, and any resemblance to actual persons, living or dead, business establishments, events or locales is entirely coincidental.

This edition published by arrangement with Harlequin Books S.A.

For questions and comments about the quality of this book, please contact us at CustomerService@Harlequin.com.

® and TM are trademarks of Harlequin Enterprises Limited or its corporate affiliates. Trademarks indicated with ® are registered in the United States Patent and Trademark Office, the Canadian Intellectual Property Office and in other countries.

Printed in U.S.A.

**Laura Marie Altom** is a bestselling and award-winning author who has penned nearly fifty books. After college (Go, Hogs!), Laura Marie did a brief stint as an interior designer before becoming a stay-at-home mom to boy-girl twins and a bonus son. Always an avid romance reader, she knew it was time to try her hand at writing when she found herself replotting the afternoon soaps.

When not immersed in her next story, Laura plays video games, tackles Mount Laundry and, of course, reads romance!

Laura loves hearing from readers at either PO Box 2074, Tulsa, OK 74101, or by email, balipalm@aol.com.

Love winning fun stuff? Check out lauramariealtom.com.

### Books by Laura Marie Altom

### Harlequin American Romance

#### Cowboy SEALs
*The SEAL's Miracle Baby*

#### Operation: Family Series
*A SEAL's Secret Baby*
*The SEAL's Stolen Child*
*The SEAL's Valentine*
*A Navy SEAL's Surprise Baby*
*The SEAL's Christmas Twins*
*The SEAL's Baby*
*The Cowboy SEAL*

Visit the Author Profile page
at Harlequin.com for more titles.

This book is dedicated to the millions of men and women suffering from PTSD. While there is no "easy" cure, my prayer is for love to ease your healing journey. xoxo

# Chapter One

"Get out of here! *Get!*" Wiley James waved his battered straw cowboy hat at the miserable beasts, but four of the llamas kept right on munching the tops off his carrots.

A fifth stared him down, then spit.

"Oh no, you didn't…"

Wiley tried charging the damned thing, but with his bum leg, he lost his balance and fell flat on his ass. Adding insult to injury, dust rising from his fall made him cough. It was early June, and his slice of northwestern Montana hadn't seen rain in a couple weeks.

His hat tumbled off in the breeze.

Frustration and sheer rage tightened his chest—not so much at his neighbor's escaped llamas, but his own situation. Six months earlier, he'd been at the top of his game—a Navy SEAL who never backed down from any challenge. Then he'd gone and done a Texas two-step with a Syrian cluster bomb and life had never been the same. Hell, he was lucky to even have his leg, but after a string of reconstructive surgeries and months in rehab, to now be stuck on this old run-down ranch instead of working with his SEAL team to do his part in saving the world… Well, let's just say he wasn't exactly thrilled with his current lot in life.

"I'm so sorry," a female voice called from behind him.

"Chris, Sabrina, Kelly and Jill! Shame on you. You know better! And Charlie—I told you no more spitting!"

The beasts stopped chewing long enough to give her a curious look, but then returned to their meal.

"Can I help?" The woman belonging to the voice stepped in front of Wiley, blocking the too-bright sun. Standing in shadow, he couldn't make out much of her besides a giant mass of red hair.

She held out her hand.

He refused to take it. "No, thanks. I'm good."

Wiley scrambled back onto his feet, but downright humiliated himself in the process. He had a cane somewhere in the house, but he was only thirty-two. No way would he consider using the thing till his eighties.

"I really am sorry about your garden."

"Me, too." It had taken weeks to get his plants to this stage, and her llamas had ruined damn near all of them in minutes. Now that he'd taken a good look at her without the sun in his eyes, he noticed the baby she held on her hip. The little guy had her red hair and even a few freckles. Her sky-blue eyes looked familiar. He knew her—he'd *always* known her. The realization that this woman was little Macy all grown up made his throat tight and chest ache.

"Henry and I will help you replant."

"Who's Henry?" he asked, playing it cool. "Your husband?"

"This is Henry. Wave," she coached the baby. "Wave hello to our nice neighbor."

The chubby baby not only flapped his hand, but grinned.

"Doesn't look like much of a gardener." Wiley fought to maintain his scowl, but it was kind of hard when faced with this level of cuteness. In another lifetime, he'd wanted to be a father. Wiley's already battered ego couldn't help but wonder why Macy hadn't recognized him. Did he look *that* bad?

"Oh—he loves digging, but needs help planting." She held out her free hand for Wiley to shake. "I'm Macy Stokes—well, used to be Shelton. Henry and I live just down the hill."

"I know. Clem and Dot's place."

Her smile faded. He cringed at being the subject of her appraisal. "Wiley?" As if coming in for a hug, she raised her free arm and stepped forward, but then seemed to change her mind and step back. "I didn't recognize you with your long hair and stubble. Dad told me you were back, but it's been so quiet over here, I thought he was wrong. It's great seeing you again."

"Likewise," he lied. What was the point of moving out to the middle of nowhere if you weren't going to be left alone? He didn't want the social responsibility of making small talk with the neighbors any more than he wanted to clean up after their nuisance animals.

The Veterans of Foreign Wars—VFW, for short—welcome committee had already been out on three separate occasions to invite him for Tuesday night poker, but he'd sent them packing. The last time in what he hoped was a definitive manner. When he said he didn't want to see *anyone*, he meant it.

He turned to hobble after his hat.

"I guess you heard about my grandfather?" Time hadn't changed their roles. She chased after him just as she had when she'd been a little girl.

"Nope. But I wish him and Dot well."

"That's just it—my grandpa died."

He paused. "Sorry to hear it. Clem was good to me. Dot, too. She okay?" Even this modest bit of pleasantry cost. More than anything, he wanted the freedom to be as glum as he liked. Pretending to be civil had proven far too much of an effort, which was why he'd chosen to hide where there were far more soaring pines than people. The ranch was twenty-five miles from town. Macy was his closet neighbor. The next closest was a good five miles down the road.

"Grandma's alive…" Though her eyes welled, Macy forced a smile and jiggled her baby. "But not especially well. A few years back, she started forgetting things—at first, leaving the teapot too long on the stove or her friends' names—but when it started getting out of hand, my mom took her to the doctor, and Grandma Dot was diagnosed with Alzheimer's. Grandpa was gutted. Honestly, I think the pain of losing her—even though she was right there with him—is what literally broke his heart."

Wiley knew he should say something. Dot used to make him oatmeal cookies with butterscotch chips. He'd loved those cookies, and he'd loved her. So why couldn't he move his lips?

He'd reached his hat, but without something to lean on, there was no way he'd be able to grab it without losing what little remained of his dignity.

"You all right?" Macy asked. She'd cocked her head, and the breeze captured her mess of red hair.

Her baby giggled when the curls tickled his chubby cheeks.

The two seemed so happy, Wiley couldn't help but stare.

"Wiley?" Never dropping her gaze from his, Macy crouched to retrieve his hat then hand it to him. "Everything okay?"

His throat constricted.

"Because if not, I'll be happy to help. If it's the garden you're upset about, it's early enough in the growing season that we can replant everything that's ruined."

"I appreciate the offer," he said, "but what I'd really like is for you to take your furry friends back to your pasture, and keep them off my land."

"Okay. Sure." Her smile faded to a crestfallen expression he wasn't proud to have caused, but also wasn't particularly inspired to change. What did that say about him? About the man he'd become? He couldn't bear for her to compare him to the fit, capable, cocky teen he used to be.

"Doing it sooner would be better than later." She needed to go *now*. Because he could no longer stomach the sight of her adorable, cherub-cheeked baby or her direct gaze or crazy-curly ginger hair. Her creamy complexion with its smattering of freckles or her full, bow-shaped lips. Most of all, he couldn't stand this new expression of hers that he interpreted as disappointment. As much as she'd admired him when they were kids, to now see the disaster he'd become must be a letdown.

Instead of leaving as he'd asked, she just stood there, staring. And then, she cocked her head. "You never wanted me to hang around with you when we were young, but you never used to be mean about sending me on my way."

"Your point?" He crossed his arms. Her stare made him feel exposed, as if she were trying to figure him out. He didn't like it.

"No real point." She shifted the baby to her other hip. "It's just been a while since I've encountered anyone quite so rude."

*Sorry*, is what he should have said. *It's nothing personal. It's me, not you.* What came out was, "I'm busy, and wasn't expecting company—especially not a herd of llamas."

"Whatever. Can you please at least help me get them back home?"

"I would, but…" Wiley had a white-knuckled grip on the porch rail for support. "Like I said, I'm busy."

"You're not busy." She narrowed her gaze. "You're just a big old horse's behind. Forget I asked." She put her fingers to her mouth and whistled. "Chris, Sabrina, Kelly, Jill! Let's go! Charlie, you, too!"

Even though Wiley had spent his entire adult life helping others in need, on this day, he stubbornly held his ground—not because he didn't want to help, but because pride wouldn't let him.

"...AND THEN HE told me he couldn't help round up my llamas because he was *busy.* Who says that?" After the morning she'd had wrestling her mischievous livestock back to their pasture, Macy was all too happy to unload on her parents who lived in Eagle Ridge—the nearest town to her grandparents' cabin and acreage. The hodgepodge A-frame and ranch combo where she'd spent her childhood was always sun-flooded and usually scented by some sort of baked good. On today's menu—zucchini bread.

"Word around the VFW is that Wiley hasn't been the same since his last trip to the Middle East." Her father, Steve, jiggled a giggly Henry on his knee.

"What happened to him?" her mother, Adrianne, asked from the dining room table, where she worked on her scrapbooking obsession. She belonged to a club, and the one-upmanship sometimes got a little out of hand.

"Guys down at the VFW say he came darned close to losing his leg in Syria. He was in one heck of a skirmish—won just about every medal a man can for bravery and valor. But he's not right up here." He tapped his forehead with his index finger.

"Now, Steve, that's not nice. We can't know that."

"I served in the first Gulf War, and plenty of the men I came home with were never the same—you hear about it all the time—think about those poor guys who served in Vietnam. Personally, when the time is right, I wouldn't mind talking to Wiley about what he's been through. I know we had our differences, but that was back when he was a teen and our daughter was moon-eyed over him. That said, I'd feel more comfortable if Macy kept her distance—especially with the baby."

"Dad…" Macy sat beside him on the sofa, and took Henry's tiny hand. "The Wiley I knew was strong, and filled with self-confidence, and maybe even a little wild— but never dangerous."

"Yeah, well, you knew him as a teen—and I didn't much like him then. Now, he's a Navy SEAL—or at least was— you don't know what kind of hell those special ops guys go through. Stuff probably straight out of the movies. As far as I'm concerned, you'd be better off safe than sorry. Just stay away."

"Is Wiley still handsome?" Adrianne asked. "You used to have the worst crush on him. Your grandparents once bought you one of those disposable cameras and when we had it developed, the whole thing was full of sneaky pics you'd taken of him."

*"Mom!"* Macy's cheeks no doubt glowed from excess heat. "That's so not true. I remember that camera, and I had lots of horse pictures, too."

"Whatever you say. You know how I love my pictures. If you'd want to launch a friendly wager, I'm sure I can find them around here somewhere."

Macy rolled her eyes. "You're acting nuts. I don't know why I even came over."

Her dad snorted. "You're here for free dinner."

Adrianne laughed. "True! And don't think you're getting out of here without telling me if Wiley's still handsome."

"He's okay." And by okay, she meant, *good Lord, was he hot!*

Macy wasn't even sure where to start.

That morning, Wiley hadn't been just easy on her eyes, but steal-her-breath-away gorgeous. His brown gaze was so intense she'd had to look away. He wore his dark hair on the long side, and judging by his scruffy facial hair, he hadn't shaved in days. And his body—*whew*. His broad shoulders barely even fit in his faded PBR T-shirt she remembered him getting when his grandpa took him to the Vegas finals.

"Just, okay?" Her mom frowned. "That's disappointing. I had visions of a romantic reunion."

"Don't encourage this," Steve said. "Do you want our girl to get hurt?"

"Oh, quit being a worrywart." Adrianne waved off her husband's concern. "Wiley's a fellow veteran. I would think you'd give him your respect."

"He has my highest admiration and thanks. One day, I'd be honored if he considered me a friend. But when it comes to giving my blessing for him to marry our daughter and become Henry's stepfather, can you blame me for wanting to be cautious?"

Macy sighed. "Hate to interrupt this charming debate, but you two are aware of the fact that at no point when Wiley ordered me, Henry and our llamas off his land did he ever once propose?"

WILEY HAD NEVER been a morning person, but his leg pain made it especially tough to get out of bed with a smile. The constant ache shaded his life in gray, and turned even cheery sun dull.

He tossed back the sheet and quilt to ease from the bed. The cold plank floor nipped the soles of his feet. Having spent the past decade on base in Virginia Beach, and in mostly hot-as-hell Middle Eastern locations, the chilly mountain starts to his days took some adjusting to.

After using the bathroom, then splashing cold water on his face, Wiley wound his way through the four-room log cabin to the kitchen. The place had been in his family for three generations, and though it had been updated with modern plumbing and electric, the hand-hewn logs held on to the original character. Age made them glow with a golden patina.

He rummaged through the fridge, but shouldn't have bothered. No food fairies had shown up in the night. He settled on a protein bar and steaming mug of half coffee, half whiskey to dull his pain.

With his second serving of fragrant, fresh-brewed java and Jim Beam, he wandered out to the covered front porch only to get a shock.

Macy was hard at work in his garden.

She'd woven her mane of wild red hair into a loose braid, and hummed while planting green beans that looked larger than the ones her llamas had eaten.

Baby Henry sat beside her, happily shrieking each time he raked his fingers through the soft soil.

The sight of mother and child both incensed and mesmerized him.

Why were they on his property when he'd told Macy he didn't need help? Why couldn't he look away from the quintessential slice of normalcy they represented? Lord help him, but he envied her ability to find joy in the simple work.

He shouted from the porch, "I told you I could handle replanting."

"Good morning!" Her pretty smile didn't help his dour mood. "Gorgeous day, isn't it? But I hear it's supposed to be rainy by tonight—which is good. We could use a good old-fashioned toad strangler."

"Why are you here?"

"Aren't you cold with no shirt? It's chilly."

She'd pulled this same crap when they'd been kids—purposely ignoring him until she wore him down to do her bidding—usually, manipulating him to give her a ride on his horse or hike to the mountaintop lookout where Dot and Clem had forbidden her to ever go alone. How many times had he almost kissed her in that spot before chickening out?

Annoyed by the fact that part of him still craved kissing her, he asked, "How is it that you're a full-grown woman, yet every bit as annoying as back when you weren't tall enough to reach my belt buckle?"

She laughed at the dig. "For the record, I wasn't *that* short, and at least I'm not lazy—still loafing around in my pj's at almost ten o'clock."

Wiley wanted to zing her back, but how could he when she spoke the truth? He never used to sleep this late. But when he had no goals beyond getting through the day, it wasn't as if he had a whole lot to wake up for.

Henry shoved a dirt clump in his little mouth, then cried in protest.

"Silly rabbit," Macy cooed while hefting the baby onto her hip. "It might look like nice, brown chocolate, but that dirt's not quite as sweet, is it?"

She marched toward the cabin. "I hate to be a bother, but would you mind if I used your kitchen sink so I can wash out Henry's mouth?"

Wiley struggled not to growl. "Help yourself."

"Thanks. You're too kind." Her blown kiss only heightened his frustration.

While Henry roared at the indignity of having his mouth

cleaned, Macy sang to the infant and hugged him and assured him everything would soon be all right. And it was. And when all that remained of his ordeal were his tear-stained cheeks and the occasional shuddering huff, the baby's smile returned.

"He's a charmer," Wiley couldn't help but note.

"Just like his momma?" Macy winked.

"Cocky much?"

"Only with smart-mouthed cowboys."

Maybe it was the whiskey making him mellow, but he couldn't hide his half smile. "You are something else. A sassy firecracker of a girl who drove me nuts, and now that you're all woman, not a damned thing has changed."

"Language," she warned. "And thank you—I think."

"You're welcome—I think." The overalls she wore were as kooky as her hair. The red long johns top clashed, yet somehow managed to only make her freckles and ample female curves pop. As a woman, the mischievous girl in her shone through, but she possessed an intriguing, all-grown-up feminine appeal from which he couldn't look away. "Does your husband approve of you showing up on another man's land first thing in the morning?"

Her smile faded. "Who said I was married?"

## Chapter Two

"Sorry," Wiley said. "Guess since you have a baby, I assumed Henry has a dad nearby."

"Yeah, well, he doesn't." When it came to discussing Macy's ex, Rex, aside from the cute rhyme, there was nothing amusing about what he'd done. He not only cheated on her during her pregnancy, but left her two months after Henry's birth. Macy's best friend, Wendy, had warned her he was no good, but Macy had refused to listen. They hadn't spoken since.

"Hey, I didn't mean to start anything." He bowed his head, and for the first time since their unlikely reunion, seemed genuinely affected by something she'd said. "I was just making conversation."

"It's not a problem. Talking about it makes me sad. I'm generally a happy person, and…" Her voice cracked, but she refused to give Rex any more power to darken her life. She swiped tears from her cheeks, then kissed Henry's dirt-smudged forehead. "Anyway, thanks for letting me use the sink. I'll finish in the garden and leave you on your own to do whatever it is you do."

"Macy, wait." She'd walked past him only to get a jolt when he reached out and touched her arm. Their contact had been fleeting, yet each individual fingerprint scorched through her thin shirt. She'd given him up such a long time ago, but her body remembered what her heart had tried to forget. When he'd left for the Navy, announcing he had no plans of ever coming back, she'd still been in high school and forced herself to move on. "Sorry I've been such a hard-ass."

"It's okay." She didn't want this attraction to him. Moreover, she didn't understand it. Her father cautioned her to keep her distance from Wiley, but the part of her that had shared seemingly endless summers with him on this very land found it awfully hard to stay away. "Henry's dad cheated on me. I had had a tough pregnancy, and we weren't...*together*...for a while."

"That doesn't give a man the excuse to step out." Was that alcohol on Wiley's breath? "If anything, you having a rough time should have brought you closer."

"Please, stop." For some crazy reason, she found it easier to be with Wiley when he was salty. This new and improved kinder—possibly drunk—version knocked her off balance. "I'm over it and I suppose, in retrospect, if I'd have paid more attention to Rex's needs, I wouldn't be a single mom now."

"You know how when we were kids, I used to razz you about everything from your shortness, to talking too much, to the color of your hair?"

"Yes. But how is that supposed to make me feel better?"

"Hear me out. The point I'm trying to get at is that as annoying as you were, I still had—*have*—affection for you. You might be a pain in my you-know-what, but you're mine, you know?"

"Oh, my God, you're awful." She left the shadow-filled living room in favor of occupying a rocker on the porch and plopped Henry onto her lap. "You've gone from telling me I'm stumpy and have ugly hair to calling me a pain in the rear."

"You totally misunderstood what I was trying to say." He'd limped after her, and leaned on the low porch rail in front of her chair. "Even though it's been years since we've seen each other, I have fond memories. You're the kid sister I never had."

*Yet another low blow.* From the first day she'd met him when she'd been six years old, she'd suffered from a serious case of puppy dog adoration. On that day, she'd announced her plan to marry him. But now that she was grown, she realized he was nothing more than a neighbor—not even a particularly good one! If that was the case, why did her pulse quicken just being near him?

"Thank you for your help in the garden. The past few months have been tough. I didn't mean to take my frustrations out on you. From here on, I guess we'll just agree to keep our distance, and—"

"Why?" Macy asked.

"Excuse me?"

"Why should we make an effort to stay apart?" For some unfathomable reason, her breaths turned erratic from just asking the question. She'd meant it in a purely platonic way, yet the girl who'd crushed on Wiley as if he'd been a hunk straight off the cover of her coveted *Teen* magazines didn't acknowledge that fact. Forging ahead even though her best course would probably be to hush, she said, "Think about it. You, me and Henry are all alone up here. Every day I struggle to care for the animals and garden and cook and still have time to spin my fleece and knit. You're probably messing with the same chores. Think how much more efficient we'd both be if we did everything together—just like we used to when our grandparents made us muck stalls and weed their gardens."

For a long time he was quiet, which made her wonder if she'd done the wrong thing in even making the suggestion.

"If you don't think it's a good idea," she finally said, unable to take any more of his stony silence, "that's okay. I mean, my feelings won't be hurt."

"Look, your idea has merit, and if I were in a different—"

"Forget I asked." Because now that he was turning her down, Macy felt stupid—ridiculous, considering she shouldn't have even asked him in the first place. But despite the brave front she put up for her parents, the truth about her daily existence was that she often felt starved for adult companionship. She hooked one of Henry's curls with her pinkie finger. She loved being a mom, but sometimes she caught herself carrying on conversations with an eight-month-old and actually expecting him to answer. "Guess I'll go ahead and finish planting, then be on my way."

"I told you I'd do it."

"Yes, you did. But I don't like feeling indebted to someone, and the fact of the matter is that my llamas trampled your tomatoes and ruined your entire row of green beans and zucchini. Since your plants were already established, and starting you over from scratch with seed didn't seem right, I dug up mine."

"You what?" He frowned. "Macy, that's crazy. It's not like if I don't have green beans and zucchini I won't survive the winter. You do realize there's a grocery store just down the mountain in Eagle Ridge?"

"I know, but—"

"Look…" He sighed. "You were honest with me about your ex, so I'm going to return the favor. You might not have noticed yesterday, but I don't get around as well as I used to. God's honest truth? My pride didn't want you seeing me in my current condition. The fact that you dug up your own garden to replace mine? Well, it's real decent of you—especially after the way I acted. And since we're now down to only one patch of beans and zucchini between us, how about we share?"

"You sure it won't be a bother?"

He scratched his head. "Forget all I said about your plan, and let's team up on our gardens—but that's it, okay? I'm not good company right now, and—"

She rose from her chair to hug him.

"Please don't say that about yourself." She'd meant for the gesture to be no big deal—a casual hug between old friends. But with the baby between them, and her past feelings for Wiley creeping in like a seductive fog, she couldn't help but long for something more. But was that longing so much about Wiley? Or her desire to go back in time to a period when life had been uncomplicated and happy, with her only cares centered around where she'd traipse after her favorite cowboy on any given summer afternoon?

What she hadn't expected was for Wiley to hug her back—fiercely, as if she were a lifeline. "Thanks."

"For what?" When she summoned the courage to pull back, she peered up at him, halfway expecting to find the answers in his brown eyes for why he'd turned so bitter. But then did she really need further explanation beyond the aggravation he must feel about his leg? And about being forced by circumstance to retire from a job that—if her dad's VFW hall gossip was correct—had been more like his life's passion?

"I'm thankful for your help with the garden—but mostly, for you being you. I've been so wrapped up in feeling sorry for myself, I never stopped to consider just how many folks have it worse than me. Raising Henry on your own can't be easy."

"It's not, but…" Did he really equate her son with his having a disability? Just when they'd taken a baby step forward in behaving civilly toward each other, why did she feel as if they'd now taken two giant leaps back? "You do understand that no matter what happened with my ex, Henry's a blessing?"

"Oh, sure. I meant that we all have our own crosses to bear." He conked his forehead. "That came out wrong. I didn't mean to imply you're not a great mom, and your baby's not cute as a button—just that it's tough enough caring for your livestock and garden on your own, caring for a baby alone must be ten times harder."

"True. But I don't dwell on the fact. I prefer to look on the bright side, which is that I've been gifted with an angel to remind me how sweet life can be."

"Wish I were able to share your optimism." He looked down. "Right now all I can see is about three steps ahead, and that's scary. I've always believed I could weather any storm, but this thing with my leg is different. From the start, it was totally out of my control—and I hate that. If something's happening in my life, I ought to be able to confront it head-on."

"I'm sorry," she said. "What you're going through—I can't imagine. But things are going to be okay. They always are."

His gaze turned cold. "Wish that were true, but it's been my experience that a lot of times, shit goes from bad to worse."

"I think you were right…" It was on the tip of her tongue to scold Wiley about cursing in front of her baby, but why waste her breath? Considering his dour frame of mind, he'd only do it again. "It's probably best if we keep to our own parts of this old mountain. All the plants I owe you are in my wheelbarrow in your side yard. I've got the roots wrapped in damp paper towels, but you'll probably want to get those in the ground sooner as opposed to later. Leave the wheelbarrow by my gate. I'll come around to get it."

Before she lost her resolve, Macy hiked Henry higher on her hip, then took off across Wiley's yard.

"Aw, hell…" She barely heard Wiley mutter. "Macy, wait!"

"Can't!" she called with a backward wave after stooping to pluck Henry's backpack-style carrier from where she'd left it in the garden.

And that was the God's honest truth. She no more trusted herself to turn around for one last look at Wiley than she did not to eat an entire plate of fresh-baked chocolate chip cookies.

He'd always represented something larger-than-life. Years before he'd been a hotshot SEAL, he'd possessed a cocky swagger. A way of squaring his shoulders and jaw that had not only mesmerized her, but alerted her to the fact that he was beyond her reach—not that he'd ever said it in so many words, but in her heart, she'd known.

Even when she was fourteen and more than ready for her first kiss, she hadn't dared hope to experience the feel of her lips grazing Wiley's. He was destined for better than her—a greatness she'd recognized even all those years ago. At the time, she'd predicted he'd one day be a famous bull rider—maybe even a movie star—and considering he had a face handsome enough to charm the devil, Macy figured Wiley would end up with a rodeo queen or a brilliant doctor or lawyer. Never in a million years would he end up with a girl as ordinary and plain as she.

And yet now, walking away from him, she recognized the tables had been turned. Oh, he was still every bit as handsome as he'd ever been. And his slight limp didn't bother her in the least. What she did find inexcusable was his attitude. She was sorry for what he'd been through—

couldn't even imagine the horror. But that didn't give him the right to abandon life. Where his gaze had once been vibrant and sparking with energy, those same brown eyes now looked dead. And that scared her.

FOR ABOUT FIVE SECONDS, Wiley considered chasing Macy, but what was the point? They'd said all they had to say—he'd spilled far more than he'd ever planned to share with anyone—let alone the firecracker who'd tormented him for as long as he could remember.

He exchanged his flannel pajama bottoms for jeans and a red plaid shirt, rammed his bare feet into socks and then cowboy boots, then headed to the garden.

The notion that Macy had uprooted her plants for him had him all messed up inside.

Who did that?

Sure, they'd been friends back in the day, but they were nothing now—less than acquaintances. Which begged the question, why had he spewed all that personal BS? And why did he now feel like crap over the fact that yet again he'd sent poor little Macy skittering as if she was Beauty and he was the Beast?

So what? Why did he care?

Maybe because that story she'd told about her cheating ex hadn't set well. She deserved better. With that crazy-colored hair of hers and freckles that looked as if angels sprinkled cinnamon atop the bridge of her button nose, she was more than pretty. In fact, there had been a point before his grandfather died when Wiley had started to look at Macy in a much different light than merely the pesky little kid from next door.

She'd been fourteen, and he'd just turned eighteen—too old for her, yet incapable of turning away from the kid-transformed-into-sexy-young-woman stealing the show at his high school graduation party.

Macy had tagged along with Dot and Clem.

He closed his eyes and saw her as plainly as if he'd stepped back in time.

The night was unseasonably warm and scented with a bouquet of feminine perfumes. A thunderstorm approached and lightning backlit the partiers making good use of O'Mally's deck. Every so often thunder boomed. Eagle Ridge had only four restaurants, but this was his favorite, which was why his parents held his party there. So many people had come that the event spilled out of the private dining room and the local band his dad hired set up on the covered stage located just off the spacious deck. The stage was two-sided, which allowed whoever was playing to perform inside or out. In the winter, a garage door closed it off from the snow, but tonight, that door stood open for the band currently performing a Bon Jovi classic.

Liquor was flowing, and Wiley's grandfather kept sneaking Wiley and his friends steady rounds of whiskey shots and beer.

"Hey, Wiley," Macy said when she left the dance floor for a cup of his mother's virgin punch. She looked different—*better*. "Excited to be out of school?"

"Hell, yeah." He couldn't stop staring. What had she done to transform herself from pain-in-his-ass to hottie? When had she gotten boobs?

"Got big plans?"

"Nah. Grandpa needs me to help on the mountain. I figure I'll do that in the off-season, then hit the rodeo circuit. You know I won my last three bull-riding events."

She rolled her eyes. "Duh—like you've only told me ten times. Get a new story."

"Kiss your mom with that sassy mouth?"

"Nope, but I wouldn't mind kissing you." She raised her chin, and the challenge in her eyes did funny things to his stomach. She'd put her long curls up, and instead of her usual T-shirt and jeans, she wore a blue sundress that made it all too easy for him to peer down at her female assets. Her mounded boobs had him not only hitching his breath, but shifting his weight to hide the instant action beneath his fly.

"You're just a kid," he mumbled.

"Not anymore." In the shadows with the band now playing a slow country song, she sidled up close—uncomfortably close. Not because he wanted her to go away, but because in that moment, he didn't want to let her go.

She escaped his hold to dance solo, waving her arms above her head, which only put more of a strain on her dress's thin fabric. Lord, her boobs were nice. How had he never noticed?

Thunder cracked.

Other guests shrieked while running inside to get out of the sprinkles promising to soon be a downpour, but she stayed.

The rain made good on its promise, and even though the band had stopped playing to move their gear inside, Macy danced to her own music, swaying and laughing with her eyes closed. As long as he lived, Wiley doubted he'd ever see a more beautiful sight. Her hair had fallen and her soaked dress had turned see-through. She wore no bra, and in the light cascading through the windows, nothing was left to his imagination.

She was no longer Little Macy, but a girl he *had* to have.

"You're wild!" he called above the storm.

She giggled. "I know."

"I've got to kiss you." Wind pushed him closer, and with

his hands on her sweet ass, he pressed himself against her, needy for release.

"It's about time."

A gust stole his straw cowboy hat, but he hardly noticed on account of how badly he wanted her. He leaned in for that kiss, but then her dad charged onto the deck and grabbed hold of the back of Wiley's shirt.

"Boy, what the hell are you doing?" To his daughter, Steve barked, "Macy, get inside!"

"Y-yes, Daddy." Her teeth chattered.

"I—I'm awfully sorry, sir. It—this, won't happen again."

"Good. It better not," Steve said. "Get out of this rain and sober up. You smell like a damned brewery."

"Yessir." In the packed restaurant and bar, the increasingly drunken crowd turned rowdy, but Wiley's brief interaction with Macy's angry father turned him sober.

Wiley tried finding Macy, but her whole family was gone.

Hours later his parents were, too—only forever.

Having had too much to drink, his father had taken a curve too fast on the slick, winding mountain road leading to their home. The car careened off a steep embankment, and according to the sheriff, his folks had died instantly.

By all rights, Wiley should have been with them, but he'd been back at the bar, shooting pool and drinking beer with his friends.

A week later, Wiley joined the Navy and didn't return to Eagle Ridge for ten long years until his grandfather's funeral—which, considering what a great man his grandfather had been, pretty much made Wiley scum. Now, four years later, the only thing that had brought him back was his bum leg. Otherwise, he would still be doing the job he loved, with the friends he loved. He sure as hell wouldn't be back on this mountain where everything he saw and touched reminded him of all he'd lost.

Not just his health and way of life, but his entire family.

It was too much loss for him to cope with, let alone understand, so he finished in the garden, then retired to the front porch with a bottle of Jim Beam. And he drank and drank until the whiskey's warmth dulled the physical and emotional pain, and Macy was no longer an attractive, vibrant woman from whom he still craved that long ago stolen kiss.

## Chapter Three

"Ever going to spill the real reason why you dragged me out here? I doubt you needed help finding just the right cucumbers for your new pickle recipe."

"Busted." Macy cringed, hating that her mother knew her so well. It was Saturday, and while her dad had stayed home with Henry, Macy and her mom strolled Eagle Ridge's farmer's market, winding their way past vegetable and fresh-cut flower and artisans' stalls. A local bluegrass band played in a cordoned-off section of the parking lot. A trio of bare-bellied, long-hair hippy-types from a local commune danced with tambourines and streaming ribbons. Sunshine and cool mountain air laced with pine and incense reminded Macy why she'd come home from Billings after Rex had gone.

It had been two days since she'd last seen Wiley, yet their simple hug—and the electric jolt she'd received from that most basic touch—had been branded into her short-term memory. As for her long-term memories? Those were a tad more complex.

Macy said, "I have a question for you that Dad's not going to like. So please don't tell him, okay?"

"Promise, my lips are sealed." Adrianne pretended to lock her lips.

"Thank you, but the last time you used that gesture,

your lock turned out to be made of Silly Putty. I still have nightmares about what Dad said he'd do when or *if* he ever sees Rex again. You didn't need to tell Dad he cheated."

"Of course I did. Otherwise, he wouldn't have understood the divorce. But that's ancient history. This time, I really won't tell."

"Hope not." Macy was skeptical, but all of her high school friends save for Wendy had moved on to the big city, meaning at the moment, her mom and Henry were all Macy had to use for sounding boards, and one of the two didn't say much beyond *goo* and *gah*. "What if maybe I was attracted to Wiley?"

"I don't understand the question." Adrianne plucked tomatoes from a bushel basket and dropped them in her paper bag.

Macy forced a deep breath. "Well, it's no secret Dad doesn't approve of him, and he's got issues, but part of me wants to kiss him so bad I can't hardly stand it." Shocked by the extent of her own confession, she covered her mouth. Cheeks warm, she said, "That came out wrong. What I meant was that he looks awfully good in his Wranglers and cowboy hat. That's all."

"Honey…" After paying for her produce, Adrianne led her to a bench tucked alongside the stream bubbling its way through the park. "There's nothing wrong with a little fooling around." She winked. "After all Rex put you through, you're entitled to some good old-fashioned noogie with a tall, dark cowboy. Which is a long way of saying, I guess I'm still confused by your question, since it's okay—even perfectly natural—if you're still crushing on Wiley."

"I know, but it's complicated," Macy said. "He's not the same person anymore. Sure, he was always cocky and had a sarcastic edge to his humor, but now something about him is so dark, and that scares me. But at the same time,

I'm more attracted to him than ever. I'd about given up on him when he confessed he didn't want me to see him with his bad leg, and…" Pain for him—for what he must have gone through—radiated through her. "Mom, I was lost. At that moment, I wanted to do whatever I could to help him. But then I noticed how dead he looked in his eyes—it was as if he hadn't just lost full use of his leg, but his humanity. Maybe this time Dad was right, and I should stay away?"

"Is that what you want?" Her mom had a way of cutting straight to the heart of the matter. "Because the way I see it, aside from those few rocky years with Rex, you've pretty much pined for Wiley since you were a little girl. Now, he's back, and yes, he might be broken, but when have you ever turned away from anyone or anything in need of extra comfort? You were always bringing in strays, and you treat Clem's nasty old llamas like family."

"They are family."

Her mom grinned, but also shuddered. "Last time that big one spit at me, I wasn't exactly thinking of giving him a nice hug. Anyway, what I'm trying to get at is this is Wiley we're talking about. Up until he left for the Navy, you thought he hung the moon, stars and every rainbow in between. Clearly, he's in need of a friend, so why would you even think of turning your back on him?"

"Because I'm scared." Macy crossed her arms. "Mom, Wiley's not just a little sad, but fundamentally changed. I can't put my finger on it, but I think something happened to him on that last mission of his that he's not talking about— and honestly, maybe I'm not strong enough to hear."

"Again?"

Monday morning, after an endless weekend spent either drunk or sleeping or working his way to each respective state, Wiley stared down Macy's llama who contentedly munched his newly planted green beans.

The animal spit at him. What was his name? Charlie?

Wiley spit back. "You might act all badass, but that sissy bell Macy's got you wearing doesn't do much for your manhood."

The llama ignored Wiley's speech in favor of taking another big bite. This time, the beast tugged hard enough that the whole plant—roots and all—came flying out of the ground. The shock of the dirt and dust in his face spooked the llama, and he took off running—only not toward his pasture, but Wiley's cabin.

Upon discovering that was a dead end, the llama bolted into the side yard. This portion of land was close to the property line, and mostly consisted of a weed-choked, forgotten rust pile where his grandfather had dumped busted fridges, cars and washing machines for decades. Also in the mix was barbed wire, and when Charlie reached it before Wiley could stop him, the animal let out a sound signaling he was in pain.

"Damn it," Wiley said under his breath, limping to the rescue as fast as his bum leg allowed. Seeing any creature hurting was awful, but knowing this big lug was a favorite of Macy's made the situation all the worse.

"Calm down…" The rusty wire had looped around the right fetlock and knee. The more Charlie struggled, the more his heartbreaking moans dragged Wiley back to another time, another attempt to avert injury that had ultimately failed.

But not this time.

Wiley clenched his jaw, working the wire loose while somehow not getting his head stomped by one of Charlie's angry kicks.

*"Hang tight, Crow, I'll have you out of here in no time."*

*"I'm already gone,"* his SEAL teammate said from between gritted teeth. *"Get out of here—save yourself."*

*"No way, man. Let me—"* BOOM!

The final bomb's concussive force killed his buddy, Michael Young—called Crow by his friends—and threw Wiley backward a good fifteen feet. The blast rendered him deaf for days—although he still had some ringing in his ears that sometimes kept him up nights. His protective gear saved him from extensive burns—at least everywhere except his leg. He had a few faint scars on his chin and left cheek, but that was nothing a few day's beard growth didn't cover.

The internal wounds hurt most. The mental images of the countless other lives taken. In the dark of night, those were the souls haunting him, clawing at his heart and mind until he damn near felt dead himself.

"There you go," Wiley said to Charlie, stroking the animal's back while taking gentle hold of his bell collar to lead him from danger. "You're gonna be fine. We'll get the vet up here to clean you and give you a couple shots and you'll be right as rain."

Wiley's soothing words earned him a grunt.

When it came to horses, Wiley would have understood this noise, but llama-speak might as well have been Martian.

Wiley led Charlie to the barn, then found a lead rope to loop around his neck, only Charlie wasn't having it. Even with his leg scratched, he dug in to the barn's dirt floor, refusing to budge.

"Looks like we'll play this your way."

He slipped the rope off the creature's stubborn head, then limped back into the sun, closing the barn door behind him. He'd long since given up on his cell having a reliable signal, so he made it to the cabin and dialed the vet's number on his grandfather's old-fashioned black rotary-dial phone. Affixed to the wall with yellowed tape was a sheet filled with numbers written in Buster's familiar scrawl. The vet's office was just one of the numbers his grandfather had jotted down for eight-year-old Wiley to use in case of emergency. The next number happened to be for Clem and Dot's—only the voice on the other end of the line was the last he wanted to hear.

"Macy..." Wiley said. "Don't get upset, but Charlie's been hurt."

WILEY COULD TELL MACY all he wanted not to be upset about Charlie, but that didn't mean she'd listen. After hanging up the phone, she bundled Henry into his car seat, then drove Clem's more-rust-than-red pickup the short way to Wiley's grandfather's cabin.

The dust from her fishtailed parking job hadn't yet settled when she leapt from the truck to pluck Henry from his seat and into her arms, then met Wiley where he stood glowering in front of the barn.

"I told you this wasn't an emergency." He tugged the brim of his straw cowboy hat. "There was no need to drive over—let alone, drive all crazy."

"Where is he?"

"In the barn, but—"

"Thanks. That's all I need to know." She wasn't in the mood to decipher what Wiley may or may not deem a serious injury. When it came to her grandfather's llamas, Macy considered them family, just like she'd told her mom.

She tugged open the heavy barn door, then paused to allow her eyes to adjust to the shadowy light.

Thankfully, the first thing she saw was Charlie, contentedly munching feed from a tin bucket. His leg was scratched from his tussle with the barbed wire, but as long as it was treated to ward off possible infection, he'd no doubt live to escape another day.

"You scared me," she said to the infuriating, yet lovable creature. She tried hugging his furry neck, but he wrestled free before returning to his meal.

"Told you he'll be fine," Wiley said from behind her. "The vet's on his way."

"Thank you."

"I'm just sorry it happened. Charlie got into Gramp's old junk pile. I'll get someone over here to haul all of it off. In the meantime, guess we should look over your fences to see how your escape artist keeps getting out."

"Sure." *We?* Wiley was the last person she'd expect to propose a group project. But now that he had, she wasn't sure how that made her feel—especially when she once again detected alcohol on his breath. Part of her wanted to be near him—no matter what they were doing. Another part felt wary. Since her breakup with Rex, she hated the way loneliness sometimes compelled her to strike up longer-than-necessary conversations with everyone from grocery store clerks to Henry's pediatrician. The last thing she wanted in regard to Wiley was to confuse neediness for attraction. "I'm free most any day, but Saturday."

"What happens then?" he asked.

"Henry and I visit Dot. You should come with us some time—I mean, if you want." The moment the suggestion left her mouth, Macy mentally kicked herself. Backpedaling, she said, "But I'm sure you wouldn't want to. Grandma probably wouldn't even remember you."

"Actually, it'd be nice seeing a familiar face. Hard to believe we're the last ones standing on this old mountain."

"I know, right?" The fact made her terribly sad, so she changed the subject. "How long ago did you call Doc Carthage?"

"Just before I got ahold of you. He was looking in on a sick calf over in Blue Valley. It'll probably be at least thirty to forty minutes before he gets out here. Want to head home, and I'll give you a holler when he shows?"

"I suppose that would work." Craving company, she'd like nothing more than to stay—maybe play cards or simply reminisce about happier times, but since Wiley had suggested she leave, did that mean that's what he preferred?

"Great," he said. "I'm sure you're busy, so—"

"Not particularly." Henry's weight made her arm muscles burn.

"Oh, well…" They left the barn to stand in the yard's warm sun.

"This is the part when you're supposed to say 'in that case, how about joining me on the front porch for a nice, cool glass of tea or lemonade?'"

He winced. "That would be the civilized thing to do, only I'm fresh out of any beverages besides water, beer and Jim Beam."

"Right about now, any of those would do." She'd meant her statement to be funny, but considering he made her feel like a nervous teenager, she realized she meant what she said. And so she figured why not venture a step further into their land of social awkwardness. "Remember the night of your high school graduation?"

"How could I forget the night my folks died?"

"Right. Sorry." She'd been angling to see if he remembered their almost-kiss, so *ashamed* didn't begin to describe how low her spirits dipped upon realizing that of course he wouldn't remember something so inconsequential in light of what happened only a few hours later.

"It's okay." He kicked a pebble near the toe of his boot.

"I mean, it's not, but you know what I mean. What part of the night were you talking about?"

Her cheeks blazed.

"Because there's an awful lot I recall besides what happened to Mom and Dad."

Was it possible he'd thought about their dance in the rain as many times as she had?

"Your daddy still hate me?"

His direct question made her laugh. "*Hate*'s a strong word, but…"

Wiley laughed, too. "Can't say I blame him. I wouldn't have been much good for you then, and I'm a whole lot worse now."

"Says who?" Her pulse roared in her ears like a jet engine.

"Common sense."

"I never had much."

"True," he admitted with a chuckle. "I recall daring you to jump off Myer's Bluff—never for a second thinking you'd do it, but you did. The water in that swimming hole had to be barely above freezing. Took me damn near an hour's worth of holding you to get your teeth to stop chattering."

She grinned. "Ever think maybe I just liked being held?"

"Talk like that—" he bowed his head, but couldn't hide his smile "—is liable to lead to trouble."

"Maybe I like that, too."

"Macy Shelton, Dot was always threatening to wash your sassy mouth out with soap, and now I remember why. You can't run around saying things like that."

"True. But I'm not running—just standing here in the sun with an old friend. What's the harm in that?" He was so handsome, looking at him might as well have been a dream. Macy didn't have a clue what had all of a sudden turned her so brazen, nor did she care. All that really mattered was that she was tired of being alone, and no matter what her father said, the fact that fortune had chosen now to bring Wiley back into her life had to be a sign.

*"Lord..."* He took off his hat, wiping his sweaty brow with his forearm. "That always was your problem. You liked playing with fire, but at least had Clem and Dot around to make sure you didn't get burned. Only now, you're a single mom, charged with this little guy's care." He jiggled Henry's left sneaker-clad foot. "Make no mistake, Macy, I'll always be your friend, but I'm also the worst kind of guy—guaranteed to bring you nothing but pain."

# Chapter Four

"You were right to call." Randall Carthage had been the veterinarian for the Eagle Ridge area for as long as Wiley could remember. His tall, wiry build didn't quite match his shock of white hair or Santa-worthy beard, which was why when he played the jolly old guy each holiday season, he had to add lots of padding to the moldy costume that had probably been used back when Wiley's dad had been a little boy. "He'll be fine, but to be on the safe side, let's give him some salve and a round of antibiotics."

"Thank you." When Macy held her baby on her hip while gifting the vet with a one-armed hug, Wiley fought a jealous pang. For an irrational flash, he wanted to be on the receiving end of her gratitude. "Charlie's a mess, but I love him."

The vet stroked the animal's side, and the miserable beast didn't stomp or spit.

Wiley asked, "How come I'm the only one who draws out Charlie's nasty side?"

The vet laughed. "Don't take it personal. Maybe he's partial to the fairer sex. Although, if that is the case, I'm not sure what that means about him getting along with an old codger like me." He winked at Macy. "Now, Wiley, if you don't mind, let's hold him in your barn overnight to keep him calm, and then, if he seems all right in the morning, go ahead and walk him over to his pasture."

"How am I supposed to do that?" Wiley asked. "The beast can't stand me."

"All right, well, Macy can put a lead rope on Charlie, and you hold the baby. Will that work?"

"Sounds good to me." Macy jiggled her son. "What do you think, Henry?"

The baby cooed.

Wiley's chest tightened.

While Macy and the vet talked llamas, Wiley recalled the last time he'd been around an infant—his friend Grady's Oklahoma housewarming. A bunch of the guys from their SEAL team had flown in for the event that had been held on Grady's family ranch. Just a few months earlier and Wiley's whole life had been different—better in every conceivable way. Holding Grady's infant son on that warm, spring day beneath the vast Oklahoma sky, he'd had his whole life ahead of him. He'd been surrounded by longtime SEAL friends and their families. Cooper and Millie. Heath and Libby. Mason and Hattie. He'd been thrilled for his married friends, but welcomed the companionship of his single friends Marsh and Rowdy. They'd all fished and grilled and downed too many beers and in general did plenty of good man shit until Mason's bossy wife told them all to shut up before they woke the sleeping kids.

Crazy how fast everything could change.

His life had been measured in tragedies—first third, his folks dying. Second third—his career going to shit. For the rest of his life, he figured he'd live alone on this piece of land that was more rock than dirt, and then he'd die.

"Who gets the pleasure of paying for my good looks and company?" Randall asked.

"Me." Macy raised her hand.

"I'll take care of it, Doc. It was my barbed wire." Before Macy could launch an argument, Wiley took his wallet from his jeans back pocket and fished out a hundred bucks. "Will this cover it?"

The vet nodded. "Macy, I'll come to your place tomorrow to give him more antibiotic."

"Thanks again."

He waved on his way to his truck. "No problem. Oh—Wiley, wonder if you might do me a favor?"

"Sure."

"If you don't mind, follow me, and I'll explain."

"Should I be worried?" Wiley asked. Maybe he ought to have asked what the favor entailed before agreeing?

"Nah…" Randall's low, throaty chuckle had Wiley thinking the opposite. At his truck, the doc walked around to the tailgate, springing it open before tugging on a wire mesh cage.

It took Wiley a few minutes to hobble that way, but by the time he'd caught up with Randall, it didn't take much to get the gist of the old man's favor. "Oh, no… If you want me to give a home to this—"

"Now, Wiley, don't you start makin' excuses before I've even explained what I need." Inside the cage was a momma hound dog and four pups that still had their eyes closed. "Some damned fool left this little lady on the clinic's front porch, and I need someone to keep her till I can find a suitable home. Your granddad used to take in strays. I figure since you've got that big empty barn, well, that would make for a whole lot of space for this beauty and her family."

"Doc, look…" Wiley shoved his hands in his pockets while searching for the right thing to say. "I would, but—"

"Nope. Stop right there. We're a tight-knit community, and in case you forgot in the time you were gone, we all help out where we can. Now, down at the VFW, there's been talk about your leg, but last I heard, a poor help-less animal doesn't care how it gets fed, just that the food comes in a timely manner."

"Randall…" Wiley had a tough enough time looking after himself. How was he supposed to care for anything else? Especially a dog and her pups?

"You'll do it? Good man!" He slapped Wiley's back. "I'm proud of you, son. Your granddad would be, too. Now, give me a hand hauling our momma to her new tem-porary home."

Wiley's stomach churned. "It's just for a few days, right? You'll put out word that she needs a permanent home?"

"Oh, sure, sure. I'll get right on it."

Together, they tugged the cage from the truck bed, then shuffled back to the barn where the vet led Wiley to a quiet corner in a patch of sun.

"Look, Henry! *Puppies!*" Macy zeroed in on the cage.

Henry stared in awe. The more the puppies wriggled and whined, the wider Henry grinned until Macy had to use her sleeve to wipe drool from his chin.

The vision of Macy and her child kneeling in dust-mote-infused sunbeams rendered Wiley incapable of focusing on anything but them—their purity and sweetness and light. His breath caught in his throat, and it took a beat to come to his senses. Macy and her boy might be a beauti-ful sight to behold, but they had no place in his carefully structured life of isolation. Since his accident, since wit-nessing death after death, he was no longer in the business of living—only forgetting.

"Doc," he said to Randall. "It'd probably be best for this momma and her pups to move a ways farther down the hill. Little Henry's already taken with the whole lot."

"Oh, no." Macy plucked up her son and backed away. "We'll be happy to stop in for visits, but between caring for an eight-month-old, an ornery llama herd, a shameful garden and a house in constant need of work, my plate's plenty full."

"That settles it." Randall patted Wiley on the back again. "Macy, I'll be 'round tomorrow to check on Charlie."

"Come during lunch and I'll have something made for you."

"Will do!" He waved on his way to his truck. After hefting a large sack of dog food from the truck bed, he left it on the dirt drive, then took off in a cloud of dust.

Cursing under his breath, Wiley hobbled to the food. He'd lost so much upper body strength, he struggled to even heft the damned bag over his shoulder, but he eventually managed, hating that the whole while he'd had an audience.

"Let me help." Macy, with that baby of hers bouncing on her hip, charged toward him.

"Do I look like such a cripple that you think you can do better with no hands?" Another fine sheen of sweat had popped out on his forehead from the strain, but he managed. With the bag near the dogs, he used his pocketknife to open it, then found an old chicken-feed scoop and shallow metal pan to fill. Pain shot up his back and down his leg, but he'd be damned if he'd let his uninvited guest see him hurting. After Macy left, there'd be plenty of time to self-medicate with a lunch of Jim Beam followed by an afternoon nap.

The whole time he worked, she stood at the barn's double doors, backlit by morning sun.

The weight of her stare hurt just as bad as his physical pain. Used to be, she'd looked at him out of admiration. Now, no doubt she felt nothing but a complete lack of respect and pity.

"Take a picture," he snapped while filling a water pan from the spigot. "It'll last longer."

"Why are you doing this?" She sat on a hay bale, positioning the baby on her lap.

Henry only had eyes for the wriggling, whining puppies and waved in that direction.

"You should probably get your kid out of here. Too many germs."

She sighed. "Practically all my life, Wiley James, you've been a horse's behind, but lately it's gotten out of hand. You show glimmers of the man I know you could be, but—"

"Did I ask for a therapy session?"

"Did I ask to get my head bit off? Don't forget, the only reason I'm even here is because you've got a dangerous junk heap in your yard."

"Oh—that's rich. Point of fact—if you'd learn to keep your goddamned llama on your own—"

Henry's little mouth puckered and he whimpered a few times before launching into full-blown tears.

She turned him around, cradling him to her chest. "Now, look what you did. He's not accustomed to raised voices."

"Great! Then, might I suggest taking your kid and prancing your sweet ass off my land!"

"You're horrible!"

"Yes, I am. The sooner that fact sinks in, the better off you'll be."

Only after she'd climbed into her truck and peeled out on a dust plume did Wiley grab a rusty hoe from the barn wall. He used it as a crutch while ensuring the dogs and Charlie had plenty of food and water. Finished, he closed the barn door to keep them all safe, then hobbled back to the cabin.

Once inside, the pain was so great the whole room felt as if it was spinning.

Still using the hoe as a cane, he made it to the kitchen, grabbed the nearest whiskey bottle, downed a good half of it, then collapsed onto the bed.

MACY WAS TOO UPSET to go home, where she'd have nothing to do but think about Wiley's poor behavior, so she turned toward her parents'. But that was no good, either, because she wasn't feeling up to answering her mom's inevitable questions regarding her neighbor. Heck, at the moment, she wasn't his biggest fan, but it didn't take a fancy psychiatry degree to see that when he'd lifted that heavy feed sack, he'd hurt himself, only was too proud—or, more likely, stupid—to ask for help, either with the feed or finding the pain meds his VA hospital doctor had no doubt sent him home with.

Where her dirt road met the two-lane highway leading to Eagle Ridge, Macy took a left toward downtown. It had been a while since she'd seen her friend Wendy—at least six months, which was way too long. Macy scolded herself for accusing Wiley of being too prideful when she was no better.

Since the divorce, she'd hidden herself on the mountain, not speaking to anyone but her parents. For as long as she could remember, her biggest dream had been to be just like her grandparents in living a simple country life, raising kids and livestock and letting the seasons dictate her work schedule as opposed to a time clock. Sure, she had all of that now, but by only half. Without love, she felt empty inside. Rex's cheating had been an awfully low blow.

She'd been too naive to have even seen it coming.

Wendy, her best friend from elementary, middle and high school, had been the one who'd told her to wake up and face reality—her husband wasn't working twenty-hour shifts at the Boise Pepsi plant. He was working that dirty blonde down at the Lookyloo Tavern, and Macy wasn't just talking about the woman's hair color.

For months after Rex left, Macy had been too embarrassed to stop in at Wendy's bakery and coffee shop, but having her behavior mirrored by Wiley didn't show her in a flattering light. Wendy deserved an apology. And after that, she'd hopefully be willing to offer advice over the new dilemma Macy faced with her neighbor.

On this sunny summer day, Eagle Ridge's Cherry Street bustled with not only locals, but the tourists staying at the campground and cabins at Blowing Cavern Lake. The old mining town was decked out in all its seasonal finery and with the Fourth of July right around the corner, red, white and blue bunting had been hung from the historic redbrick buildings' porch rails. A wide wood-plank boardwalk lined both sides of the street and hanging baskets of petunias and lobelia and ivy decorated every lamppost and column.

With no parking to be had near Wendy's shop, Macy pulled in front of the candy shop, hopped out, then took Henry's stroller from the truck bed so she could plop him into the seat. She rolled him closer to the taffy-pulling machine hard at work in the candy store's front window.

It seemed like a hundred years ago that she'd stood with Wiley in this very spot. Her grandmother had forced him to hold her hand so she wouldn't get lost. Now, after smelling booze on his breath twice at odd times of the day, Macy couldn't shake the feeling that he was the one who was lost—only in a much more serious way than running off to the far end of the boardwalk.

Henry giggled at the machine's gyrations.

"Funny, huh?"

He clapped.

She wished the sweet moment could be shared with his father, but then what would that have accomplished? She couldn't make her ex love their son any more than she'd been able to make him love her. Last she'd heard, he'd run off with his gal pal to Florida, which left Macy feeling broken and not good enough—a bad place to be when she had such a blessing in her son. For him, she needed to be strong. While she would never forget what Rex had done, or understand how he could live with himself for abandoning his only child, she had to at least learn to place the blame for their breakup on his shortcomings rather than her own.

Past the bookstore and three antique shops and a T-shirt shop that also sold assorted souvenirs and sundries, Macy stood outside Wendy's pride and joy—The Baked Bean. A year earlier, Macy had helped her friend load the flower boxes and put a fresh coat of yellow paint on the wrought-iron tables and chairs. On a busy day like this, Wendy would have called for emergency help, and Macy would have run right down to make mochas and lattes and double-shot espressos.

Today, however, she stood on the threshold, unsure about even going in. The inviting smells of coffee and fresh-baked cookies and scones tempted her, but it was Wendy's surprised gasp upon seeing her and Henry that drove her inside.

Upbeat bluegrass played over the shop's sound system, providing the perfect soundtrack for the way Macy hoped the reunion would go.

Wendy passed a tray of chocolate cupcakes to her part-time helper, Alice, then darted between customers to give Macy a much-needed hug. "It's about time you came to see me."

"I'm sorry, I…" Tears stung her eyes at the memory of their ugly last exchange of words.

*How dare you accuse my husband of cheating? The only reason you're saying any of this is because you're jealous I got married and had a baby first.*

Shame flushed Macy's cheeks. Where did she start to make amends for the horrible, unfounded accusation?

"Look at you…" Wendy took Henry, holding him out for a better view.

He'd always been a happy baby, and he grinned now with Wendy's light jiggles.

"You're so big, and have your mommy's pretty blue eyes."

"Wendy," Macy said. "I owe you a huge apology, and—"

"You don't owe me a thing. I'm sorry your fairy-tale prince turned out to be a royal scumbag."

That made Macy laugh and hold out her arms for another hug.

"I still have Henry's playpen in back. As you can see, Alice and I are swamped. Mind helping out for a bit, and then we can talk?"

Just like that, their friendship was back on track.

With Henry content in a sunny corner, alternately cooing over the toys Aunt Wendy had long ago bought him and charming the customers, Macy worked the coffee machine, filling orders as quickly as they came in. Within thirty minutes, the crowd thinned to a manageable trickle, at which point, Wendy passed Alice the reins, then tugged Macy to the backroom to make more cookies and have a proper chat.

Henry had fallen asleep, and Alice promised to let Macy know the second he woke.

Once Macy and her oldest friend caught up on each other's family news and town gossip, she wasn't surprised when Wendy broached the subject of Macy's pesky neighbor.

"Well?" Wendy asked after popping a cookie tray in the oven. "Are you ever going to tell me about your reunion with Wiley?"

"I'd hardly call it a reunion—more like a catastrophe." She delivered the short version of their encounter. "I get that he's hurting, but he acts like a grumpy old bear with a thorn stuck in his paw."

"Then you're not back to practicing writing *Mrs. Macy James* like you used to in tenth grade?"

"Um, no. He's horrible. Just when I think we could at least be civil, he goes and says something even more outrageous or offensive than the last time we talked. My dad thinks I should give him a wide berth."

"And your mom?"

Macy rolled her eyes. "Already picking wedding invitations."

Wendy winced. "It's a little soon for you to be back at the altar, isn't it? How long has your divorce been final?"

"Six months, but our marriage was over before then. And thank you for taking my side. Even if I was in the market for male companionship, Wiley is the last man on earth I'd choose."

# Chapter Five

"You're the most stubborn, obstinate, downright unpleasant creature I've had the misfortune of stumbling across in a good, long while—and that's saying something, considering your owner."

It was pushing ten in the morning, and after sleeping late, the last thing Wiley needed was more grief from Macy's stupid llama.

Charlie stared Wiley down before treating him to a hiss and spit combo, then some crazy grunt loud enough to make the pups whimper.

"Feeling's mutual, buddy..." Wiley struggled to get a guide rope around the beast's neck and eventually succeeded.

His back and leg still hurt like hell, but as he'd been taught through his SEAL training, if you have a job, do it.

No excuses.

He refused to use the four-pronged cane he'd been sent home from the hospital with, so he once again needed the hoe for leverage while opening Charlie's pen, then tugging him toward the barn door.

After pushing and pulling the damned creature to the gate between his grandfather's property and Macy's, Wiley slipped off the guide rope and encouraged the llama with a light pat to his ornery ass to be on his way.

Judging by his gallop, Charlie felt right as rain and didn't suffer any lingering pain from his previous day's injury.

Wiley wished he could say the same for himself.

He hobbled back to the barn to check on the momma and her pups.

"You didn't eat much," he said to the hound. He topped off her water and food, then moved both bowls close enough that she could snack without having to upset her suckling brood.

When he rubbed between her ears, she gave him an appreciative few licks.

"You're a good girl." Because stooping hurt, Wiley pulled over a hay bale to perch on. "What's the problem? You don't like Doc's food?"

She cocked her head. Lord help him, but her soulful brown eyes stirred something he hadn't experienced in a long time—the desire to do a worthwhile task that didn't involve sitting around feeling sorry for himself.

"Tell you what…" He gave her another rub. "I'm about out of the proverbial dog that bit me, so how about I grab you a treat while I'm in town."

She wagged her tail.

MACY PUT THE VASE of wildflowers she'd plucked from a nearby meadow in the table's center, then stood back to admire her handiwork. She'd covered the kitchen table in a green-and-white-striped cloth, then set two place settings using her grandmother's rose-patterned wedding china and good silver. Alongside each plate were salads made from the season's first lettuce and tomatoes, as well as rose glass tumblers filled with fresh-brewed iced tea.

It wasn't every day she had company for lunch and she looked forward to Doc Carthage's visit—all the more so since Charlie seemed fine. The last she'd checked on him, he'd been happily grazing in the pasture, surrounded by his *angels*.

"What do you think?" she asked Henry, who sat in his high chair, working over a teething biscuit.

"Arrrghuulah!" He bounced and kicked, and as always, her heart melted from the sight of his smile.

"You are too cute," she said in a singsong voice.

He grinned all the more.

The house smelled cheesy-wonderful from the lasagna she'd made that morning, and every wood surface shone from polishing.

The cabin might be small, but every inch was filled with love—from the whitewashed walls to the wide-plank oak floor and low beamed ceilings. Antique curio and china cabinets held her grandmother's treasures and built-in bookshelves framing the river stone hearth cradled her grandfather's beloved books.

When the crunch of tires on gravel alerted her that her guest had arrived, she gathered Henry in her arms, then bounded to the front porch to greet the vet.

Macy was all smiles until she caught sight of Doc Carthage's passenger.

Why in the world had he brought Wiley?

"Hey, little fella." Upon exiting his truck, Doc made a beeline for Henry. "I swear he's gotten bigger since yesterday."

"He sure feels like it," Macy said with forced cheer. Yesterday's encounter with Wiley had been more than enough for her. Never had she come across a man who was more downright uncivilized—well, not counting her ex, but then that was a whole 'nother story.

Wiley took his time easing from the truck, clearly favoring his leg, but taking great pains not to show it.

"Look who I found out in his yard, tending that junk pile." The vet slapped Wiley's back. "I figured if you're anything like your grandma, Macy, you made plenty enough to share. And if Wiley's half as bad a cook as his grandpa, he needs all the good home cooking you can spare."

"Yes, sir," Macy said with forced cheer. "Grandma always taught me the more the merrier." Although Macy was pretty sure that in Wiley's case, the old saying didn't apply. "Wiley, you're welcome to join us."

"Thanks." He didn't look any happier to be there than Macy was at the intrusion.

"You two go ahead and get started." Doc Carthage waved on his way to the pasture where he'd spotted Charlie. "I'm going to check on my patient, then I'll be right in. Macy, girl, whatever you cooked smells good enough that my stomach's already growling."

It was on the tip of Macy's tongue to beg the vet not to go, but it was too late. He was already gone.

Wiley cleared his throat. "About yesterday. Sorry."

"Save it." She turned her back on him to head inside.

There was another place to set and salad to make. She had no time to stand around listening to an apology that didn't come anywhere near reaching Wiley's dark eyes. His hair was too long, and he needed a shave, yet his raw good looks took her breath away. As much as she currently hated him, she'd always pined for him, even loved him, which made his current salty behavior all the harder to bear. Oh sure, she didn't *love* him, as in true love, but she felt the kind of love that came from years of companionship and togetherness and deep-down caring that refused to go away just because she dearly wanted it to.

"Really." He limped after her, which made her feel bad when he was the one who'd misbehaved! "I am sorry.

And hungry. Whatever you made smells delicious. I never would have come, but—"

"You shouldn't have." She spun to face him. "But since you did, wash your hands, then make yourself useful by sitting down and holding Henry."

For the longest time he stared at her as if he wasn't quite sure what to make of her new take-charge demeanor, but then a smile tugged at his lips and on the way to the kitchen sink, he shook his head. "Damn if you aren't still a pistol."

"Don't curse in front of the baby."

"Yes, ma'am." He washed his hands, then grabbed for Henry, but then backed away, as if he'd changed his mind. Afraid he might drop him? Macy respected him more for swallowing his pride to admit to at least himself that there could be a potential problem. He sat at the table, stretching out his bum leg, then held out his arms. "Want to deliver him to me?"

Macy did.

But when Wiley held her son as if he were as exotic as a three-headed calf, Henry pouted, huffed a bit, then fell into a full-blown wail.

"I didn't do anything," Wiley said.

"That's the point." Macy didn't want to get close enough to Wiley to recognize his old familiar scent, but for the sake of her son, she cautiously approached, taking the baby from him, only to turn Henry around so that he faced Wiley. "Hold him like you mean it, otherwise, he'll be scared. Like this…" She bit her lip while positioning Wiley's arms around Henry.

The mere act of touching the cowboy brought back so much she'd rather forget—the electric awareness that years earlier she'd chalked up to raging teen hormones was still there. The simple brush of forearm to forearm, fingers to fingers made her whole body hum. The simple touch reminded her how long it had been since she'd been with a man—if ever, considering the fact that she no longer considered her ex to be anything more than a self-centered man-child.

"How's this, little fella?" Wiley's voice had turned hoarse. Could he be as confused as she?

"If you're sure you're okay with Henry, I'll grab an extra place setting and make your salad."

"I don't need a salad—or anything special. A paper plate will do."

"Over my grandmother's dead body." As soon as the words were out, Macy regretted them. Being back in her grandmother's house sometimes made it easy to forget Dot no longer lived on the mountain. Macy imagined her out in the garden or off berry picking, instead of being in a nursing home. "Well, I don't mean *dead*, but you know—"

"I get it. And if you want to go to the trouble, thanks."

"You're welcome."

For the longest time, she stood there, unsure what to do with her hands or pounding heart. But then she turned to take the lettuce and tomatoes from the refrigerator's vegetable bin, trying to ignore the discomfort of being near Wiley.

As efficiently as possible, she washed and dried the lettuce, then tore it into bite-size pieces. She cut a small tomato and added it all to a china bowl.

When she turned to set Wiley's salad on the table, the sight of him bouncing her son on his good leg was mesmerizing. Henry's grin was huge—as was the trail of drool on his chin—but that didn't matter. A funny tightening warred in her chest. She wanted to stay mad at Wiley, but how could she when he gave her son pleasure?

"He's really something," he said. "You did good, Mace."

"Thank you." She took an extra plate from the china cabinet, then silver utensils from her grandmother's wooden chest.

"Your husband was a damned fool—sorry for cussing, but it's the truth."

A pinecone-sized knot lodged at the back of her throat, so instead of replying, she nodded.

"I am sorry for yesterday. Sometimes the pain is so much that I get a little out of my mind—it's not an excuse. Just the truth."

"Have you told your doctor that your pain meds don't work?"

"Don't take them."

"Why not?"

He shrugged. "Lots of guys get hooked. I'd rather just deal with the pain."

"But don't you see that if you're hurting bad enough to lose your temper and drink, then you're not really dealing with anything at all?"

"Look…" He sighed. "I'm doing all right today, so can we please change the topic? I found a guy willing to take some of the scrap metal in my yard, so I spent part of the morning loading it up. I've gone so soft, it's gonna take a while, but I figure I need the exercise."

"Would you like my help?" Her heart ached for him— for the boy she used to love and the man she didn't yet know. He used to be a maverick—wild and free, roaming all over this mountain without a care for anything other than where his next adventure may lead.

"Nah, I can manage."

"I'm sure, but like we talked about before you slipped back into your hard-ass routine, maybe life would be easier for both of us if we shared the tough stuff."

"You just broke your own 'no cursing around the baby' rule."

Macy tossed her head back, clasping her suddenly throbbing forehead.

"Just saying…" He shocked her with the sort of mischievous grin he might have used on her grandmother when he'd been caught with his hand in the cookie jar.

Did she strangle or hug him? "You're so confusing. Yesterday, you were out of your mind—ugly and just plain mean. And now, you're all smiley? No. Not gonna work, Wiley. I need consistency in my life—not more crazy. You don't make sense."

"You think I don't know that?"

She closed her eyes and forced a deep, calming breath. This was Wiley, her conscience reminded. He wasn't some random, unstable stranger, but a longtime friend who needed help.

Yeah, but as her father would be all too quick to point out, did that help have to come from her?

"Mmm-mmm, it smells good in here." Doc Carthage creaked open the front door. "Chasing after that ornery crew of yours worked up an appetite."

"Grandpa had a way with them." Macy slipped her hands into red oven mitts to take their meal from the oven. "I swear they know he passed, and miss him as much as the rest of us."

"Wouldn't surprise me," the vet said. "Over the years, I've seen some pretty strange things—in fact, just read a story that darn near choked me up. There was a rescued dog in Italy named Fido who was so loyal to his master, he continued to meet his bus for fourteen years after the man's death. Folks came from miles around to watch that poor dog wait for his best friend."

"That's a horrible story." Macy set a trivet on the table, then placed the steaming lasagna atop it. "So, so sad."

"Agreed." He took a seat at the table and placed his

white cloth napkin on his lap. "I'm just making a point that Charlie could very well be missing your grandpa."

"I'm lucky to not be missing a few fingers," Wiley noted. "He sure doesn't like me."

"Can you blame him?" Macy asked.

Doc Carthage laughed until he coughed.

Henry caught the laughter bug, and giggled.

"I thought we were buddies," Wiley said to Macy's son. "And now, you're yukking it up at my expense?"

As if on cue, Henry blew a raspberry.

Wiley returned the favor.

Macy settled her little comedian into his high chair, then finished putting the meal on the table. Thank goodness Doc had found humor in her accidentally blurted statement, because she hadn't meant it to be funny. Wiley's moods turned on and off like a light switch. Was it any wonder Charlie was wary?

Lucky for Macy's nerves, the rest of the meal passed pleasantly enough. It warmed her heart to see both men devour her cooking. She used to love trying new recipes for Rex—at least until he'd stopped coming home to eat them.

"That was delicious," Doc Carthage said when he'd finished. "Since you did the heavy lifting by making all of this, how about letting me and Wiley clean up?"

"You're sweet to offer, but I'm sure your talents could be put to better use helping animals than washing dishes."

"Go on, Doc." Wiley stood. "Get back to work, and I'll handle things on this end."

"You're a good man, Wiley James. Charlie might not cotton to you, but I sure do." After much manly backslapping, and a hug from Macy, Doc Carthage resumed his rounds, which left Macy in the once again uncomfortable spot of being alone with Wiley.

Sure, Henry was with them, but at a time like this, a napping eight-month-old didn't do much to ease tension.

When the vet's truck reached the end of her short drive, Macy said, "You don't have to help."

"I want to." He turned to head back into the house, but struggled walking.

"Have you been pretending to be normal for Doc Carthage?"

He grunted.

Macy sighed. *Here we go again.* Any second now, Wiley's dark side would make an appearance.

She caught up with him at the table, where he'd grabbed two plates on his way to the kitchen sink, but his leg locked and he stumbled. Both pieces of her grandmother's wedding china crashed to the floor, each shattering in dozens of pieces.

"Shit, Mace..." He tried kneeling, but couldn't. The strain on his drawn mouth made her heart ache for him. "Sorry. I know how much that china means..."

"It's okay." She stepped in to help.

"I've got this." Still trying to lower himself, he gestured her away.

"No, Wiley, you don't. But that's all right." She took a chair from the kitchen table and placed it before him. "Here, use this to pull yourself up."

He did, and then hunched over the kitchen counter, looking like a sad shadow of his former self. Tomato sauce splattered his jeans and plaid shirt and cheeks.

At the sink, she dampened a dishcloth. She'd clean Wiley first, then the floor. But when she touched the cloth to his face, he flinched.

She ignored him, daubing at twin red splotches on his cheek.

The set of his lips was grim, as was his lightning-quick grasp of her wrist. "I said I didn't need help."

"But you do." When their gazes locked, her lungs refused to take in air. With her face only inches from his, she realized they hadn't been this close since their almost-kiss the night of his graduation.

He leaned forward, shocking her by pressing his forehead to hers. "I *can't* need help." He straightened, leaving her shockingly bereft without his touch. "It's a man thing. You wouldn't understand."

"Try me."

He took the rag from her, then used the chair for leverage on his way down to clear the broken china. "I am sorry about this. Your grandma told me how she bought it piece by piece."

Macy remembered the story. As a young bride, her grandmother had purchased a saucer or bowl or plate each time she'd gone to the grocery store as part of a special store promotion. "She had stories to go along with each new find. My favorite was one of the serving bowls that she'd earned the money for by selling jam."

"She made the best huckleberry jam I've ever had. Still have any?"

"There are a few jars tucked away. If you play your cards right, I might be willing to part with one."

"That's a great offer, but I've never been good with cards. I'm sure she's got a recipe around here somewhere. Why not make more?"

"I could, but that would require picking huckleberries that aren't yet in season."

"Always excuses from you." He winked.

"Always more indecipherable mood twists from you."

"I'm trying, okay?"

"I appreciate your efforts, but again—it's *me*. We've known each other forever, so please stop feeling like you have to try. I'm not asking for perfection. Just civility."

## Chapter Six

Against his wishes, or even better judgment, Wiley accepted a ride from Macy back to his house.

Upon exiting the truck and climbing the cabin's stairs, he gripped the porch rail tight enough until she drove away that he could no longer feel his fingers.

The pain was so intense he feared passing out. Putting on a good show for Macy and the doc had cost dearly.

Wiley stumbled inside, grateful that when Doc had met him in the driveway to coerce him into joining Macy's lunch party, he'd already brought the morning's liquor run prizes as well as the dog's food inside.

After opening the Jack Daniel's and taking a few big swigs, he felt fortified enough to mix yogurt into a bowl of the new high-dollar puppy food the feed store clerk recommended for the nursing momma.

He grabbed a more compact fifth of whiskey to stash in his back pocket, then used his trusty hoe for support while carrying the food to the barn.

"How're you doing?" he asked the pretty girl, gritting his teeth while setting the food in front of her, then picking up her water to fill.

The day was sunny and chilly with a brisk north wind, but inside, the barn felt calm and warm. Sunshine streamed through the gaps in the plank walls his and Macy's grand-fathers had built.

After placing the water in front of the dog, he lowered himself to the hay bale he'd placed alongside her, then reached for his whiskey, taking a nice, long pull.

"I had quite a day," he mentioned, noting that the puppies still hadn't opened their eyes. "But then I'm sure you did, too. Poor Macy has her hands full with one baby, but you've got five." He took another swig, welcoming the alcohol's mental fog. "Always thought I wanted a big family, but with this bum leg, I can't ever see myself making much of a dad." *Glug, glug.* The more he drank, the better he felt. The pain was still there—but different. No longer screaming, but calling for his attention in a normal conversational tone.

Didn't make sense—how he refused to take pain meds he knew worked because he was afraid of getting addicted, yet he drank more than ever. Sucked that this was what his life had come down to—choosing between two addictions.

He leaned forward, rubbing the silky fur between the hound's ears. The dog gobbled her food, drank some water and now seemed to have a tough time staying awake.

"Go ahead and take a nap, pretty girl." He finished off the bottle, then chucked it into a metal trash barrel—at least he'd tried. The plastic bottle twanged against the barrel's lip, then bounced onto the plank floor. "Hell, I might join you."

He tipped sideways, resting his shoulder against the barn wall.

His chin drooped to his chest.

"Macy's grown into a helluva fine-looking worm, don't you think?" His sluggish brain caught up with his grammar snafu and he laughed. "I meant woman—no offense if you prefer worms."

Dust motes danced in lazy sun.

What he wouldn't give to once again dance with Macy the way they had the night of his graduation—before her dad had interrupted and certainly before his parents' accident.

If he wasn't plastered, he'd have much more to think on the subject, but right now, all he wanted was a nice rest.

*WHERE THE HELL am I?*

Wiley was slow to wake.

His head felt like a concrete block, and his body even worse. The barn was cold and dark—creaking under the pressure of a gusty wind. The night carried too many uncomfortable noises.

His brain told him branches scratched the old tin roof, but his runaway pulse said rats—worse, the enemy, creeping in for an ambush. Something thumped against the far wall. He tensed, automatically reaching for the SIG SAUER P226 9 mm that was no longer there.

Forcing deep breaths, he covered his face with his hands.

He was home. Montana. The only thing even remotely threatening on this mountain was his sassy neighbor and her nuisance llama. He had a shotgun for the occasional bear or mountain lion, but he hadn't seen signs of either since he'd been back.

He glanced down to find the momma hound staring, her dark eyes shining in the gloom. "What are you doing awake? Cold?"

He rubbed behind her ears. She felt warm to the touch and wasn't shivering, but just in case, he'd return to the feed store in the morning to find a barn-safe heater.

"Okay, well…" After a sharp exhale, he nodded toward

the door. "I'm going to bed for whatever's left of the night. I'll bring more of your special grub in the morning."

In the house, he drank enough to help him fall asleep.

In the morning, he woke hating himself even more than he had the night before.

This cycle had to stop. But how?

His physical therapist had given him exercises, but they'd only worsened the pain. In his whole freaking life, he'd never been more out of shape both mentally and physically, and he didn't have a clue what to do about it.

The fact that he drank too much was a given.

When he'd been on active duty, he'd consumed four- to five-thousand calories a day. Now, he doubted he even got a third of those—not that he needed them for what little activity he managed. Regardless, drinking all of his daily calories sure as hell was contributing to his problem.

While his mind wandered to the previous day, he rubbed his aching chest. The last thing he'd wanted had been to join Macy and the doc for lunch, but it turned out to be an okay time. Good eats. Even more enjoyable company— at least until the pain had taken over, and he'd once again made a fool of himself by falling and breaking Dot's china.

He'd make it up to Macy, starting by unearthing his laptop, then heading down to the local coffeehouse to launch an online search to hopefully replace the plates he'd broken.

But first, he fed the momma dog who had gobbled her yogurt mix faster than he had Macy's lasagna.

In town, he stopped by the feed store and picked up a heat lamp that was usually used for chickens, but he figured it would work for a dog family, too.

He had a hell of a time finding a parking spot for the coffeehouse, but as far as he knew, it was the only place besides the library that had public internet, and he sure wasn't risking a chance meeting with Mrs. Runyan—the librarian who'd caught him smoking with his friends while they'd been flipping through breastfeeding books, looking at boobs. Not one of his prouder moments, but at fifteen, he hadn't had many.

Overseas, he'd acquired a taste for Turkish coffee and The Baked Bean surprised him his first day back in Eagle Ridge by making it just right.

Wiley left the truck in front of the post office, then stashed his laptop under his arm for the hike to the coffee shop. His leg hurt like hell from the effort of walking as normally as possible. Pride was a real bitch, considering his doctor had offered to authorize a handicapped parking permit.

He was sweating by the end of the block. Two blocks later, he'd need more than coffee to put him back on an even keel.

*Focus*, he told himself. *Finish the job.*

At the coffee shop's counter, he ordered his usual and a couple blueberry muffins from the too-cheery woman behind the counter. She wore her long dark hair in a ponytail. A sunflower barrette held it in place.

"This is your third time here in two weeks. That makes you a regular, and I know we've met before, but remind me. I'm Wendy."

*I'm not in the mood for chitchat.* "Wiley."

"Of course—" The size of her already toothy grin doubled. "You're the Wiley who used to go to Eagle Ridge High, aren't you?"

"One and the same." *And I'd prefer to sit down instead of rehashing glory days.*

"Must have been the hair and whiskers that threw me off." Her eyes narrowed. "If you're on the mountain, I'll bet you've seen Macy. Isn't her baby a charmer?"

"Yeah. How much do I owe you?" He nodded to the coffee she held and the muffins she'd already put on the plate sitting on the counter.

"No charge. You're practically family."

"Thanks, but—" he withdrew a ten from his wallet "—I pay my own way."

"Sure." She handed him his coffee, and he prayed for the strength to maintain his grip long enough to make it to the corner table he'd claimed by leaving his computer on top. Her eyes narrowed as if she was trying to figure him out. He must have bored her, as a few seconds later she tallied his purchases, then punched the figure into the cash register before the drawer popped open and she delivered his change.

He planted two bucks in her tip jar, then grabbed his muffins and walked away. With his back to her, he gritted his teeth, focusing for all he was worth to walk the way he used to—the way she no doubt remembered.

It took about twenty minutes to find Macy's gift, then input his credit card information for the Des Moines antique shop owner. He downed his coffee and food before answering a couple emails from Rowdy and Marsh, then made the excruciating march to his truck.

On the way out of town, he stopped at the liquor store where thankfully the same clerk who'd checked him out before wasn't working.

His last stop was the grocery store for more of the momma hound's yogurt. He should have grabbed food for himself, but what was the point when as soon as he fed the hound, he planned on drinking his way straight to bed?

"YOU'RE NEVER GONNA guess who just came in."

"Who?" Macy set her cell phone on the kitchen table—surprised she even had service—putting it on Speaker for

Wendy's call. She'd need both hands for feeding Henry his pureed peaches. She'd spent the morning sorting bundles of Peruvian alpaca and llama fibers that she'd use for spinning and then knitting and weaving the sweaters she sold at pricey ski-resort boutiques. Her grandfather had made do with the fiber from his own herd for his woven art pieces, but when a certain Hollywood starlet had been spotted in a tabloid wearing one of Macy's sweaters, her business had taken off, necessitating the need to import fibers from all over the world.

"Your cranky neighbor. Boy, was he a cool customer. Talk about a dark stare—looked like he wanted to kill someone."

*He must have been in pain.*

"I've never seen anyone gulp Turkish coffee as fast as him. Then he ate a pair of muffins as if he was starving."

*And hungry.*

"He's spooky hot, but in a tortured way. I agree with your dad. Wiley's no good. You need a Hallmark sort— you know, someone good with the whole wine and roses and candlelight routine. The only thing Wiley's probably good at is making a woman wish she'd never met him."

A problem, considering Macy was already at that stage, yet still magnetically drawn to him. No matter how much he'd changed, he was still Wiley James, the toughest, most badass cowboy she'd ever known. He'd tamed horses deemed lost causes. He'd tossed hay bales as if they were tissue paper. To see him reduced to a man so devastated by pain that he could scarcely control his emotions didn't sit well.

He didn't need her scorn. He needed help. But what could she do for him? Wiley needed round-the-clock nursing care.

Maybe it would be cheaper to find him a wife?

No. Even though he'd proven he was no good for her, Macy wasn't sure she could stomach the thought of him being with another woman so soon after he'd limped back into her life.

"Macy? You there?"

"Yeah. Sorry. I'm multitasking. Wiley's a mess to be sure, but I think with time, he can rebuild his life."

"Like Steve Austin? *The Six Million Dollar Man.*"

Grimacing, Macy asked, "Watch much retro TV?"

"Don't knock it. From what I can tell, the seventies weren't as bad as everyone says. And my cable's so crappy that's practically my only channel besides sports, news and the local channels—which are usually only playing sports or news."

"You're lucky to have cable. It's like the Stone Age up here." Which was just as well. No TV meant more time to spend with Henry and the garden and her knitting.

And Wiley?

The mere thought of him revved her pulse. Being near him produced the same sort of chemical rush as the last time she'd spotted a bear—cautious excitement. Her runaway pulse didn't care that he was no good for her, or that her mind should be focused on a hundred other more important tasks than figuring him out. Her only productive thought was that she had to help him. But how?

*What if you married Wiley and took care of him?* That six-year-old girl who'd once proposed? Yeah, she was clearly still lurking in Macy's subconscious. The idea was crazy. Yet that buttinsky girl kept talking. *You've dreamed of becoming Mrs. Wiley James since like forever...*

Wendy said, "I dated a guy who's a satellite company rep. Want me to have him give you a call?"

"No!" Macy had been so deep into her strictly theoretical fantasy about her old friend Wiley that she'd forgot-

It only took a few minutes to store her gardening tools and the hose in the shed, then a few more to clean up, run a brush through her hair and change into a pretty yellow sundress and her favorite red cowboy boots.

She added lip gloss, then grabbed the diaper bag, keys, her purse and Henry.

"Am I nuts for doing this?" she asked her son, while grinding the old Ford into Reverse.

He was too busy eating his plastic key ring to answer.

"I sure will be glad when you finally talk." At the end of the dirt drive, she turned toward Wiley's. "But then again, if you turn into a chatterbox like Aunt Wendy, maybe I won't."

At Wiley's, she parked in the shade and rolled down the windows. For the few minutes it would take her to grab Wiley, Henry would be fine in his safety seat—especially since he'd never be out of her view.

She hummed as she bounded up the porch steps, surprised to find the front door closed. On warm days, Wiley's grandfather had always left it open, just closing the screen door.

The screen stuck, but an extra hard tug got it open so she could knock. She tried for a good few minutes, but Wiley didn't answer. He'd parked his truck near the barn, so he had to be here.

Worried, she tried the door to find it locked.

Frowning, she checked on Henry to find him still making a snack of his keys, then looked for her neighbor in the barn.

"Wiley?" she called into the barn's gloom.

The momma hound barked.

"Hey, there, pretty girl. How are your babies?" Not wanting to leave Henry for too long, she gave the dog and

puppies a quick pat, then dashed back outside, closing the
barn door behind her.

She checked the garden, junk pile and even glanced out
at the pasture only to find no Wiley. When another knock
on the cabin door garnered no results, she climbed back
behind the truck's wheel, still planning on visiting her
grandmother, but not feeling as good about it.

Where could Wiley be?

*If he was your husband, you'd know...*

Cheeks flushed from the ridiculous idea, Macy sped
away from Wiley's grandfather's cabin as fast as the old
Ford truck could go.

WHAT WAS THAT NOISE? Were they under attack?

Wiley bolted upright in bed, grabbing the rifle he kept
alongside him.

It took a while for his heart to stop hammering. Not
only was he alone, but he wasn't in Kobane. The sound
wasn't incoming artillery, but knocking on the front door.

"Wiley? It's Macy! You in there?"

He groaned.

"I want you to come with me to see my..."

Her voice was muffled, making her last words impossible to hear, but he got the gist. Her dad wasn't his biggest
fan, which meant she probably wanted him to join her on
a visit to Dot's rest home.

Hell.

Emotions warred within him like mini grenades. Part
of him wanted to tag along. He'd liked and respected Dot.
But considering how much pain he'd been in after that
morning's trek to town, he'd downed an awful lot of rot-
gut, which had left him in no shape for civilized company.

Hiding behind the silly lace curtains one of his grandfather's lady friends had put up what seemed like a hun-

dred years ago, Wiley swallowed the knot lurking at the back of his throat. Part of him wanted to call out to her.

No.

A guy as messed up as he had no business with a perfect girl like Macy. Look at her, crossing the dirt yard to the barn. Her pretty yellow dress clashed with her red boots and fiery hair, but somehow her freckles and curls tied it all together in a fashion statement only she could pull off.

All he had to do was take a few steps to his right, unlatch the dead bolt and then give her a holler. They'd have a nice chat with Dot. Maybe share an even nicer meal after.

*Move*, his heart dictated.

His feet refused.

He'd had far too much to drink, and as a result, wasn't thinking straight. Dot had Alzheimer's, and there wasn't anything *nice* about that. How would it feel to see a woman who'd been like a second mother, only to have her not even recognize him?

*How would it feel?*

Like shit.

His stomach seized, damn near hurting as much as his leg. More than anything, he wished for a do-over to turn back the clock. He'd not only avoid that cluster bomb, but bring back his parents and grandparents—Macy's, too.

He'd do everything different, starting by doing something about the fact that little Macy had grown into a fine-looking young woman a helluva lot sooner than the night of his high school graduation.

He closed his eyes.

When he opened them, she was gone.

He limped to the kitchen for a fresh bottle, then used his hoe as a crutch to hobble outside to drink with his temporary dog.

# Chapter Seven

Macy did visit her grandmother, but far from her chat bringing much-needed solace, it only reinforced the fact that Dot was already gone. At the same time, it left her desperate to help Wiley before he, too, vanished from her life as swiftly as he'd reappeared.

Which she didn't understand.

Hadn't she already had more than enough sorrow and heartache? Why invite what would inevitably bring only more trouble by purposely inserting herself in Wiley's life?

As for marrying him to be able to help him full-time? That was just silly.

Take today for instance. The brutal truth was that when she'd stopped by to invite him to visit Dot, she was guessing there hadn't been anything wrong with him, and he hadn't been suddenly swept off on a new military mission or even to a friend's. Most likely, he'd been in his cabin not just purposely avoiding her, but everyone. What did that say about his mental state? About how messed up he'd become?

She tightened her grip on the truck's wheel.

Instead of veering toward the mountain, toward home, she kept moving forward to her parents. More specifically, her mom. She needed to sort through her thoughts about Wiley, and she needed her mom's wisdom.

In fifteen minutes, she'd reached her mom and dad's outstretched arms and gladly stepped into their hugs.

As always, there was an initial flurry of excitement over how much Henry had grown, but then her father returned to the garage where he'd been tinkering with the lawn mower and Macy and her mother gravitated toward the dining room where her mom sat at the table, surrounded by images of her and Steve taken on their Christmas cruise.

"This is a nice surprise." Adrianne picked up her scissors, painstakingly cutting a photo of Steve pretending to surf in front of a big wave backdrop. "With all you've got going on up on the mountain, I didn't figure we'd see you till this weekend."

"I missed Grandma, so I went to see her early." Macy took Henry from his carrier to hold on her lap.

"I'm almost afraid to ask how she is. Dad and I went Tuesday, and it wasn't good. She thought he was a tax collector and I was trying to recruit her into a religious cult."

"I wondered where she'd got that," Macy said with a sad smile. "She thought the same about me."

"So sad." Macy's mother shook her head while pasting her *surfing* husband on a glittery wave sticker she'd already placed on the current page in her vacation scrapbook. "My friend Shirley—you remember her? From scrapbooking club?"

Macy nodded.

"She went through the same with her mom, only she was out of state. Toward the end, Shirley rented an apartment to stay closer. Broke her heart. When her mom passed, she struggled with a fresh batch of guilt about feeling relieved to no longer have to see her mother in such a wrecked emotional state."

"Mom?" Macy jiggled Henry on her knee.

"That's me."

Macy tried not to roll her eyes. "I'm being serious."

"So am I…" Adrianne grinned.

"Whatever—I need to talk to you about something."

"Let me guess—Wiley?"

Macy winced. Was she that transparent? "Okay, well, his behavior isn't exactly normal. As much as I hate to admit it, Dad was probably right about Wiley having issues. I can tell he's in a lot of pain, and I'm pretty sure he's drinking—*a lot*. But then, every so often, he shows these teasing glimpses of the kind of man he could be, and I…" Eyes watering, Macy pressed her hands to her chest.

"You want to help him?"

"Yes, but could that be a bad idea? By being around him any more than I have to, am I asking for trouble?" She smoothed Henry's hair.

"Honey…" Adrianne left her chair to hug Macy from behind. "I'm hardly an expert on these kinds of things, but the way I see it, as long as we've known him, Wiley might as well be family. Just like you would never consider abandoning Grandma, I'm assuming you feel the same about Wiley. Am I right?"

Macy nodded.

"Then here's what you're going to do." Adrianne drew out the chair beside her daughter. Once settled, she took Macy's free hand, delivering a reassuring squeeze. "Unless your heart tells you something different, you're going to be the charitable, loving woman I know you to be and help your friend however you see fit. Now, I'm not telling you to launch some scandalous affair that—"

"Mom!" Macy snatched her hand back to cover at least one of her flaming cheeks. "That's not what I meant." *But maybe that's what I want? Only I'm afraid of getting hurt all over again?*

"It's okay if you were. Just take it slow."

"I'm not interested in anything but friendship. I'm still too messed up about Rex to even think of being with another man." At least that's what she kept telling herself. But she'd been so lonely, and Wiley did need help… What could it hurt to get a little closer?

"Perfect."

Macy wished for a shred of her mother's confidence in the situation. Wiley's slightest touch reawakened a curious hunger for him that she'd tucked away and thought forever buried. But now that he was back, she wasn't strong enough to deny it. The giddy teen in her craved him like M&Ms. But why? If they were to build something beyond friendship, would it even be real? Or would she be using him as a bridge to reconnect to happier times?

"You look pretty intense," her mom said. "Relax. As long as your heart is in the right place, and you mean well, whatever help you decide to give Wiley will be good for him."

"I know." She leaned in to give her mom a hug, not letting go until Henry squirmed between them.

She still didn't have a clue what to do when it came to Wiley. Or, maybe her answer was to not do anything. To wait until the universe sent her a sign.

IN THE PAST WEEK, Doc Carthage had dropped off an abandoned goat, a one-eyed orange tabby, a skinny old nag named Lulu that preferred the far end of the pasture, and now Doc presented him with a three-legged Yorkie.

"Blinkie," Doc said, "lost his leg in a mouse trap, and his family got laid off and had to move to find work. Well, when they couldn't find a new apartment that takes pets, they asked me for help finding this fella a good home. Considering what a fine job you've done with our momma hound and Lulu, the horse, damned if your name wasn't first on my list as a potential new doggie parent."

While coming up with a way to tell the vet no, Wiley stared across the yard.

"Have you named the momma yet?"

"I thought her being here was only temporary. Didn't figure she'd be around long enough to even give her a name."

"Oh, oh right." Doc held out the hamster-sized dog, but Wiley wasn't taking it. No way. Not happening. "I'm sure I'll find a good home for all of them soon, but until then, I'd appreciate you holding on to them for a while longer."

Wiley cocked his head. "Man to man, finding homes for any of these lost souls isn't high on your agenda, is it?"

"You're good." The vet chuckled, setting Blinkie on the top porch step, then jogging to his truck and hopping behind the wheel. Before Wiley had even made it to the porch, let alone tried chasing after him, a dust cloud was all that remained of the doc's visit.

"Well, hell..." Wiley removed his battered straw cowboy hat to give the ridiculous mutt a hard stare.

It was shivering on an eighty-degree day.

The cat sat on the porch rail, using his one good eye to give the pitiful creature a lofty look of disdain.

"What am I supposed to do with you?" Wiley plucked up the dog.

Blinkie licked his fingers.

"Thanks, but I don't need dog kisses."

As did every other critter on the mountain these days, the dog ignored him to keep right on licking. He'd also stopped shivering.

Wiley sighed. "I can hardly take care of myself, so I'm not sure what I'm supposed to do with you."

The pup settled into the crook of his arm with a shuddering sigh.

"You do know you have no business being on this mountain?" Wiley backed onto the nearest step, relieved to be off his leg. "You'd make the perfect, bite-size morsel for damn near everything out here."

Apparently becoming a bear or mountain lion appetizer wasn't high on the dog's worry list as he'd already fallen asleep.

Swell.

It didn't take a rocket scientist to figure out Doc's game.

It was a classic kill-two-birds-with-one-stone scenario. Not only was Doc steadily clearing his veterinary clinic of broken misfit *toys*, but to his way of thinking, he was giving an equally broken man something meaningful to do. Only Wiley didn't need a barn filled with animals to keep him occupied when it already took damn near all his strength to keep an adequate liquor supply.

"Blinkie, let me teach you about the fine art of dulling whatever ails you." Wiley made it into the house intent on pouring a drink, but then figured why even dirty a glass when he could down it straight from the bottle.

He'd just unscrewed the cap when he heard tires crunching on the dirt drive.

He set down the whiskey, and exhaled. "Blinkie, you seem like a good guy, but clearly Doc came to his senses and realized you need a lot better parent than me."

Wiley made it out to the porch to make the handoff only to find Macy instead of the vet.

A string of mumbled curses passed his lips.

She waved, then after barely having time to kill the engine and put the old truck in Park, she'd dashed out from behind the wheel to dart up the porch stairs, crushing him in a hug. "Thank you!"

"For what?"

Blinkie squeaked his displeasure at having been smooshed.

"Oh—*ooooh*. Look at you." Stepping back, Macy cupped the dog's face. "You're a doll." She looked up at Wiley. "Where did he or she come from?"

"He—and who do you think?"

She laughed, taking the dog from him.

The exchange brought her too close, and he lacked the wherewithal to process how he felt about her bare forearms brushing against his. She made him feel off balance—and for a guy with only one good leg, that wasn't ideal.

"Henry's going to be so excited." Before he could ask what she was thanking him for, she'd run to the truck to show the baby the dog. "Wiley, come look! They're adorable together!"

His trusty hoe leaned against the porch rail, but he opted against using it. Call it pride or vanity or just plain pigheadedness, but he couldn't bear showing Macy one more sign of weakness. He'd rather she remembered him the way he used to be, back when he had something to offer.

He made it down the steps without additional support by keeping a firm hold on the rail. Turned out he needn't have bothered putting on a solid front for her, since she hadn't once looked up from her son and the dog.

"Look at Henry's face. He's enthralled."

Wiley finally made it to the truck, and couldn't deny that the combination of the kid's drooling grin with the dog's mini-fox-like features proved a potent force on anyone's cute-meter. But having spent a large chunk of his life as a SEAL, *cute* had never been a priority.

"Wish I had room in my life for a dog," Macy said.

Inspiration struck. "Be my guest and take this one. You'd be doing me a huge favor, and I'm sure Doc wouldn't mind since all he wanted was for the mutt to find a good home."

"I shouldn't…" Her expression read wistful longing. If she'd been a trout, she'd have already checked out his fly. All he had to do now was set the hook and reel her in.

"Look at him. He needs a woman's touch. He'll be miserable around here. Besides, Doc already brought me a horse, goat and cat to go along with the dog family living in the barn."

"They're still here?" Her eyes widened in surprise. "Thought Doc said the hound and her pups were only your temporary houseguests."

"Thank you. That's what I told him, but I think he was trying to pull a fast one, and all along knew he was never coming back for them."

"In his defense, you do have that great big beautiful empty barn just begging to be filled."

"Whatever." He ran his hand through his too-long hair, suddenly self-conscious about his outer shell. On the inside? He looked even worse. "Think Henry would get a kick out of seeing the pups?"

"Of course."

"Come on." He grabbed Blinkie. "Let's head to the barn. I'm sure the momma will enjoy the company. The goat's in the side yard. You didn't hear me say this, but I think he needs a friend. As for Lulu, the horse, she enjoys my company about as much as your Charlie." *Please, let my leg hold up long enough to get to the damn barn without too much pain.* To his surprise, he was enjoying Macy's visit. The sunshine. Even the baby and miniature dog. But how long until his leg gave out? Until the pain transformed him back into a beast? He'd made a career out of trusting his body. Now that the trust was no longer there, Wiley felt like a cheap knockoff of his former self.

"Want me to have my friend Wendy look on Craigslist? I'm sure someone around here has an extra goat or two."

"Just one—and no thanks on the help. I'll ask Doc next time he's around. How is Charlie by the way?"

"Good. As feisty as ever." She went on to explain how Charlie and his ladies tried getting into her garden, but she'd stopped them in time.

Wiley needed to keep her talking. He needed her mind focused on anything but him, and his struggle.

"When Grandpa was alive, Charlie followed him like a faithful old dog and was always getting treats. I'm guessing he expects the same from me, but lately, Henry has taken more of an interest in him and wants to pet him. Well, you can guess how that's going. Charlie spit at us both and I'm not having it."

"Don't blame you." They'd made it to the barn, where Wiley was able to lean against the door. Sweat beaded his forehead.

"Look, Henry! Remember the puppies?"

Wiley couldn't help but watch in wonder as Macy knelt alongside the momma hound, teaching her son to be gentle with his touch. Sometimes during a deployment, Wiley's team had come across families. More often than not, they'd been caught up in a shitstorm. But then there were occasions before or after a mission, maybe while just traveling from point A to B, when he'd caught glimpses of a father teaching his son or daughter to ride a bike, or a mother braiding her daughter's hair. A husband and wife holding hands while watching the sunset. Those moments stayed with him—trapped like lightning bugs in a jar.

They'd made him yearn to one day find that particular brand of not just happiness, but a place for his lonely soul to call home. But now, with his leg a mess, he felt like only half a man. What would he even have to offer a woman? Especially one as vibrant as Macy.

He missed being part of a family.

What happened to his parents was never discussed.

Only a handful of the men he'd served with even knew he'd now lost everyone he'd ever loved. No one realized what a hole that had left inside. As a result, he'd poured everything into serving his country. And he'd done a good job. But now what? His country no longer had use for him, and as far as he could tell, no one else did, either—except for Doc Carthage who viewed his barn as a pet motel.

"Have you named her yet?" Macy gazed up. Bathed in the sunshine filtering through the wood plank walls, she and her son looked so angelic it took Wiley a moment to catch his breath, let alone comprehend her simple question.

"I, ah, haven't. How about you and Henry do the honors?"

She laughed. "I'm not sure you want an eight-month-old tackling that big of a task. He's liable to name her Gaa."

"I see your point. Okay, you do it."

"Let me think…"

The hound looked content enough to purr from Macy's attention.

"I've got it," she said. "Pancake."

"No."

"Why not?"

"Maybe the better question is why? That's gotta be the stupidest dog name ever."

"Here's why—Henry and I had pancakes for breakfast and when we were leaving the house, I thought I'd gotten all the syrup off from cleaning Henry's mess, but turns out I was wrong, because Pancake just licked more from my wrist."

Her story was so *out there* that damned if Wiley didn't

find himself smiling again. "All right, you've convinced me. Pancake, it is."

"*She* is," Macy corrected.

In that single moment, with Henry giggling amongst a pile of puppies and Macy smiling his way, something happened in Wiley that he didn't quite understand. His chest tightened with what he could only identify as a pang. A soul-deep yearning for that elusive, invisible string tying him to the rest of the world. Sure, he'd belonged to his SEAL team, and they'd formed a family of sorts, but that hadn't been the same as his folks or grandfather. Or the way Macy held her hand to the crown of Henry's head, petting the infant's shock of red hair.

Just looking at mother and child told him they were a unit. And suddenly, more than anything, he once again wanted to belong. Without his SEAL family, without his real family, he had nothing. And he found that fact deeply, profoundly troubling.

Macy asked, "Where'd you go just now?"

Wiley shrugged, then pet Blinkie, who'd once again crashed in his arms. None of that mushy stuff was shareable with her. Besides, even if he did tell her, why would she care? He'd been a total ass to her since the day of their unexpected reunion. "You never did tell me why I deserved that running thank-you on the porch."

"Duh? The china? I can't believe you found two plates to replace the ones that were broken."

"Oh." He'd forgotten. Was his drinking affecting his memory? He needed to stop—soon. "Glad you liked them. I know it's not the same, but…you know."

She left Henry with the puppies to join Wiley for a hug. "Thank you. The gesture was incredibly thoughtful."

"You're welcome." Of course, the hug was only meant

as a casual gesture on her part. So why had his pulse taken off at a gallop?

"How could I not?" She was still holding him. And his leg hurt like a son of a bitch. But somehow, the only thing that mattered was the way her soft curves molded against him even though he still held the dog in the crook of one arm. Wiley had held his fair share of women, but never had one fit just right.

On autopilot, he dipped down, wanting with his whole being to kiss the crown of her head. He stopped just short, though, close enough to breathe her in. She smelled like a strawberry plucked from the garden. The scent took him back to shared picnics with their mothers competing over who made the best shortcake. So much history stood between them. Enough that holding her should have been the most natural thing in the world. But far from it, he didn't know what to do with his hands that kept creeping closer to the sweet curve of her behind.

Even worse, her eyes widened as if she anticipated more. She even licked her lips and then held her breath.

Lord help him, he wanted more, too. But before he went and did something stupid like kiss her, he backed away and cleared his throat.

He set Blinkie on the barn floor where the mutt stood at Wiley's feet, looking up expectantly as if he was waiting to be picked up again. "Glad you liked the plates."

"You already said that." Macy frowned. Had she craved that kiss as much as he had?

"You know how it is." He whirled his finger next to his head. "All this fresh air must be messing with my mind."

"I'll bet that's exactly your problem."

"Who said I had a problem?"

She'd just opened her mouth for no doubt her next

smart-mouthed retort when she eyed her son fisting dog food into his surprisingly big chops. "Henry, no!"

In a flash, she'd left Wiley to clear the little guy's pie hole. The puppy chow must have been tasty as the poor kid seemed about as bereft as Pancake when Macy took away his food.

She hefted Henry into her arms, rocking him until his cries faded into the occasional offended huff.

"Remember when I dared you to eat a dog biscuit?" Wiley asked. He hadn't thought of the incident in years. They'd been at the Eagle Ridge feed store around Christmas, standing in an endless line with Buster and Clem. They'd both been bored, so Wiley had taken a jumbo holiday bone from a promotional bin and presented it to Macy for a dare.

She made a face. "My burps tasted like chicken-flavored cardboard for a week."

"Boo-hoo. At least you didn't have to pay for the damned—sorry, *darned*—thing. It was three bucks."

She rolled her eyes.

Blinkie yipped at Wiley's feet. "I can see where this could become a problem." Wiley used what precious little strength he had to bend from his waist to scoop up the dog. Back in his hold, the annoying yipping stopped.

Macy laughed. "I'd say you two are a match made in heaven."

Wiley shot her a dirty look. "Pretty sure the zoo's visiting hours are about over."

"Oh, don't revert back to Grumpy Wiley. I'm just teasing—at least about the love match. You might not love him, but Blinkie looks smitten with you."

Wiley sighed.

"Take it as a compliment. Animals seem to know you're good people, which tells me all your huffing and puffing has been nothing more than a smoke screen you've thrown up to hide your real problem."

"And I suppose, *Dr. Phil*, you're going to tell me what that is?"

"Wouldn't take a PhD in psychology or whatever fancy degree he has to know you're understandably bitter. Life has delivered some incredibly tough blows, but if you'd let me in, I could—"

"Whoa." He held up his free hand. "Stop right there. I'm not open to becoming anyone's charity case." Wiley was so offended by her casual assessment of his truth, that he turned his back on her to head for the cabin. He'd check on the goat and Pancake later—stupid name for a dog. As for the cranky old horse? She could spend the night in the pasture.

"Wiley, wait—"

Wiley kept right on walking.

## Chapter Eight

"Don't even think about holing up in that dreary cabin, Wiley James." Emboldened by her vow to help Wiley dig himself out from under the weight of his depression, Macy wasn't about to let him run off before he heard what she'd come to say.

"Too late!" He'd reached the porch steps, probably hurting himself by taking them too fast.

"Hold on, baby," she said to her son before launching into the full-out run that allowed her to beat Wiley to his door. Out of breath, she blocked his passage. "You've become a grumpy old bear with a thorn in his paw. Why won't you let me help you get it out?"

"And just how do you propose to do that? You gonna try more animal therapy, like Doc? Maybe wave a magic wand to put me back on my SEAL team? But hell, if you can do that, why not take me back to the real good old days when my folks and grandpa were still alive and I was a halfway decent bull rider? Now, I doubt I could even climb on a horse."

"Stop."

"No, Macy, you stop. I'm not a project for you to take on, but a flesh and blood man who's had everything I've ever loved jerked away. How you gonna fix that?"

She didn't have a clue, but hoped her hurt stare cut right

through him. The faint, boozy aroma of his breath should have sent her running, but the attraction she'd felt for what seemed like forever was too strong to fight.

When she couldn't answer, he came back with, "That's right, you can't tell me your magical solution. So why don't you take your smiley baby back home and leave me to stew."

"No." She raised her chin. With her whole heart she suspected her old friend was all bark and no bite. He talked a mean game, but only a good man set up a heating lamp for a dog and worried if his new goat should have a friend. Wiley needed her. Moreover—she needed him. She could fix him from the outside in, and then, just as she'd dreamed all those years ago, the two of them, and now Henry, would all live happily ever after.

He would never hurt her like Rex. *Never.*

"Excuse me?"

"You heard me. I'm not going anywhere until you agree to let me help."

"Didn't we just go over this? There's literally nothing you can do."

"What about cooking? You've definitely lost a few pounds since I last saw you."

"I'm a grown-ass man." He set Blinkie on one of the wide wooden porch rockers then folded his arms. "I know how to work a can opener."

"You can't live on canned goods alone. It's not healthy."

"Then how'd my granddad make it to ninety-three on pork and beans?"

"Wiley, please…" Macy bowed her head, resting her chin atop Henry's curls. Her son patiently lounged in her arms, surprisingly not upset by this latest squabble, but watched them as if the silly grown-ups provided good entertainment.

"What? What the hell do you want from me? This afternoon, this little bit of civility, it's all I've got. I get the feeling you're trying to mold me into some version of the kid you used to know, but a whole lot of water's flowed under that bridge. Even if I'd left the Navy whole, I still wouldn't be complete. I've seen and done things…" He stopped when his red-rimmed eyes shone with unshed tears.

"I don't care what happened," she murmured, swallowing a huge lump in her throat. Her heart ached for this strong, proud man. "And okay, so yeah, maybe I did think just hanging out with you could possibly solve part of your problems, but don't insult me by acting as if I thought mere conversation could ever make you whole."

"Then why are you here? Why won't you leave me alone?"

"Because I *can't*!" Her vehemence startled Henry into tears. She soothed the baby, but refused to stop what she'd only just started with this stubborn, infuriating, fascinating man. Call her crazy, but she truly believed she had something special to offer. If he'd drop his guard long enough to let her in, wonderful things might happen. He'd stop drinking and start living. "Talk to me. We're two reasonably intelligent people. Let's figure something out to make your life better. Your doctor had to have given you stretching exercises, right? Maybe I could help with those? I don't mind cooking extra when I make meals, and we could both use each other's help in our gardens. There's summer canning to do and fences to maintain. After all of that, I still have to spin yarn and knit a gazillion more sweaters before autumn. The sheer volume of work around my place makes my head spin. How can you not feel the same?"

"Honestly?" He laughed, then plucked up the dog to practically fall into the rocker. "I do my best not to feel at all. Makes life a whole lot easier."

"That's unacceptable." She sat in the rocker beside him. "There have been a few times I thought I've smelled alcohol on your breath. Have you been drinking to escape?" Her heart pounded while waiting for his answer.

He leaned his head back and sighed, all the while rubbing the scruff of his newest dog's neck. "What if I have? Last I checked, I'm over twenty-one."

"You also have a father who accidentally killed your mom and himself while drunk driving. I would think of all people, you'd be the last person to drown your sorrows in a bottle, considering most of your earliest sorrows were caused by one." She'd gone too far and said too much.

Macy tensed, waiting for Wiley to blow, but he didn't.

Instead, he hunched over the sweet little dog and released a strangled, guttural cry that hurt far worse than any of his sharpest verbal arrows.

Henry had drifted off to sleep, so she left the porch to tuck him safely into his car seat. She covered him from the approaching night's damp chill, left the truck door open, then jogged the few feet back to the porch, to Wiley.

She knelt before him, twining her arms through his in an awkward hug. The dog had stilled, eyes wide, leaning into the wall of Wiley's stomach.

Wiley's sobs went on for as long as he needed, and when they finally stopped, she was still there, combing her fingers through his hair and rubbing his back and pressing soft kisses to the top of his head.

"Everything's going to be okay," she promised even though she feared nothing could be further from the truth. As much as she'd fantasized about the two of them sharing a future, about her being the one to fix him, could she? Fear that she couldn't knotted her stomach, caution lights flashed in her heart, but she refused to give up—

not when she'd come so far. "I'm here. You don't have to go through this alone."

"I'm sorry," he finally said. "I shouldn't have broken down like that. I don't know what's wrong."

"You're human." She was back on her knees in front of him. "There's not a thing in the world wrong with you— there would be if you didn't show pain. I can't imagine what you've been through. I'd be honored if one day you'd tell me, but if that day never comes, that's okay, too. All that matters is getting you better—or, at least as good as you can be."

He nodded.

It brewed a special brand of torment to witness one of the toughest guys she'd ever known surrender so easily, but she suspected nothing about his acquiescence had come easy. He'd warred with it as much as whatever action he'd seen that had led him to this dark place.

"I have to ask," she said, "have you been mixing alcohol with your pain meds?"

He shook his head. "I don't take any meds."

"Why not? Your doctor prescribed them, didn't he?"

"Sure, but they're too addictive."

"Are you kidding me?" It took a huge effort not to conk his head. "But you think alcohol is so much safer?"

"I know a lot of guys who got hooked on drugs. Booze seems like the lesser of two evils. You don't understand."

"You're right. I don't." She forced a deep breath, drawing strength from the long-familiar sounds of early evening on the mountain. The wind high in the pines. A hawk's lonesome cry. "When's the last time you had medication, and did it work for you then?"

"I don't know. I guess back at the hospital I took some. And sure. It worked fine. But the last thing I want is to become another veteran statistic. On top of everything else, it'd be too—" he tossed up his hands "—cliché. Pathetic. Sad. Take your pick of terminology. It's all pretty much the same."

"What if it's not? What if you take your meds exactly like your doctor prescribed, and surprise—you actually feel good enough to take back your life? How amazing would that be?"

"I can't take the risk."

"But drowning yourself in booze night after night is acceptable?"

"When are you leaving?" He tried getting up, but she pushed him down.

"Stay here." She yanked open the creaky old screen door to find more of a nightmare than she could have imagined.

Littering his kitchen island were dozens of booze bottles of varying shapes and sizes. Some full, some empty. All telling a story she didn't want to know. But now that she did, she felt responsible to rewrite.

She fished beneath the sink for trash bags.

This far from town, most folks burned their garbage, but she planned on dragging every last memory of booze out of the cabin and straight to the city dump.

A plastic jug of cheap vodka was first to go down the sink's drain, then whiskey, then scotch, then she started over with tequila.

"Hey! What the hell do you think you're doing?" He tried stopping her, but she wasn't playing. When he grabbed hold of her arm, she pushed him away.

"Saving your rotten life is what I'm doing. You can thank me later."

"Screw you! My life is fine." He began gathering the unopened bottles she hadn't yet touched.

"Then how come you cried for a good thirty minutes

out there on the porch?" She hooked her thumb in that general direction.

He didn't have an answer.

"Do you think you're already an alcoholic? Or are you drinking to mask pain?" She pressed the heels of her hands to her forehead. "Is there a difference? I'm hardly a professional. I don't know."

Hugging the bottles as if they were a lifeline, he shook his head, then nodded. "I don't think I'm an alcoholic. I just know that times like now, when my leg hurts so bad I could scream, the only thing that makes it bearable is to drink—a *lot*."

"Have you had anything lately?"

He shook his head. "But I want to."

"Try something else for me instead."

"I can't take those pills. What if I start and can't stop?"

She abandoned her latest bottle to wrap her arms around him, resting her cheek against the wall of his solid chest. His heart hammered in her ear.

When he wrapped his arms around her, her body hummed, as if on a soul-deep level she'd come home. But Wiley wasn't home. He wasn't anything more to her than a dear old friend who needed help. But if that was the case, why did she clutch him tighter? Why was she terrified that if she loosened her grip for even a moment, he'd be in peril? And then so would she, because somehow their lives had become irrevocably intertwined. Or maybe they'd always been, but time and distance and a lousy marriage had stolen what they'd once been and *finally*, this was their fresh chance.

Which made no sense, because if she was honest with herself, aside from their lone hot dance on his graduation night, that's all there'd ever been—at least on the surface. But for her, there had only been him.

Rex had been a poor substitute.

"Where is your medicine?" she asked.

He released her to take her hand, leading her toward the small bathroom. From the kitchen, she'd had a view of Henry, still sleeping in his carrier on the truck's front seat, but from in here, the view was blocked, which made her antsy.

Wiley opened a medicine chest and removed a large bottle. "I'm supposed to take two of these, three times a day. But that seems like a lot, you know?"

"Sure, but, for the rest of today—maybe tomorrow, could you please try my way? Your doctor's way?" The room was too cramped for comfort. Not only couldn't she see Henry, but under the glare of the bare bulb mounted to the ceiling, she saw all too close just how changed Wiley had become. His dark hair had always had a slight curl, only now that it had grown longer, the waves nearly brushed his shoulders. His facial hair was well on its way to becoming a mountain man's dream, but if she had her way, he'd be clean-shaven.

The room smelled of the Irish Spring soap he'd always used, which made her mind drift to him standing in the claw-foot tub for a shower. Better yet—lounging in that tub, with all of his muscles on display.

Macy shook her head. This wouldn't work. She was here to help the man—not molest him.

"I should check on Henry." With the pill bottle in hand, she returned to the main room where she found her son still sleeping. If she didn't want him up all night, she should wake him, but not quite yet. Not until she'd convinced Wiley to at least try dealing with his pain in a different way.

Wiley had followed and now stood behind her, not touching her, but close enough for her to feel every solid inch of him. He was still a powerful man. She couldn't imagine what he must have been like before the accident that had for all practical purposes taken his leg.

"He's a good-looking kid," Wiley said. "I actually got a kick out of watching him with the puppies today."

"Me, too." *Are you going to try to stop drinking, Wiley?* The question was right there but she was afraid to ask. Had she already pushed him too far, too soon?

As if he'd read her mind, he asked, "Is this whole meds thing open for negotiation?"

"Depends." He was still behind her, and it took every shred of her willpower not to turn around and hold him. Kiss him. Beg him to let her into his heart and never let go.

"I'm starving, and the directions say to always take them on a full stomach. Think you could wrangle me up something to eat? I'm sick of protein bars and ramen noodles."

"Of course, I'll cook for you—anything you want."

The only thing she wouldn't do was let him sink back to that dark place where he'd almost been lost. And the beauty in saving him? The fact that she'd also be saving herself. She'd once and for all prove Rex had been the one with the problem—not her.

No way would fate bring her the perfect man, only to have her heart break all over again.

## Chapter Nine

The relief was palpable.

Wiley sat at Macy's kitchen table with Henry chilling in his high chair next to him and he felt lighter, yet stronger. It was crazy. Thirty minutes before taking the pills, he'd been in agony.

Now, he was free.

*Flying.*

For the first time since leaving the hospital, he was able to be himself. There was none of the booze's confusion, no bad aftertaste, no thick tongue. Just peace. Gone was the sensation of his body warring against him.

He rose from the table in a fluid motion. His leg wasn't as strong, but the stiffness and sharp pain didn't have him tensing in anticipation of looming agony.

"Sit down," Macy said from the stove where she stirred a pot of chili. Blinkie sat at her feet, hoping for a handout. The food smelled good. The ground beef and tomatoes and onions. Everything had taken on a kaleidoscopic glow. "You're supposed to be resting."

"I've been resting. Now, I want to run—hell, dance." He slipped his arms around her slim waist for a turn around the room.

The dog barked.

Henry shrieked and clapped.

Macy laughed. The happy sounds quenched Wiley's thirsty soul. He hadn't realized how much he'd craved happiness and good cheer. He never planned on living life as a crusty old hermit, and now, he no longer had to.

"Take it easy," she said. "That medicine said no working machinery, driving or heavy lifting."

"Guess it's a good thing you're light as a feather." He stopped dancing to lift her. Granted, back when he'd been on active duty, he could have bench-pressed her a hundred times before breakfast, whereas now, he swiftly set her down, but this was at least progress. It gave him a starting point and a new goal to work toward: *carry Macy around her cabin*. Check.

"Stop." She gave him a light push toward the fridge. "Since you've got so much energy, how about grating the cheese? You'll find a brick of cheddar in the side door, dairy compartment, and the grater's in the cabinet to the left of the stove."

"Yes, ma'am." He easily found both, and soon they sat around the table, laughing over the simple meal of chili with cheese and saltine crackers.

He'd given the dog a cracker, and Blinkie slinked off to the quilt Macy had puddled on the floor for him to use as a temporary bed.

"Slow down," she said midway through the meal. "You're eating like you've been starved."

"I have. As good a cook as you are? I'm that bad."

Her gaze narrowed. "Wiley… The change in you…it's… it's like a miracle. You sure you're okay? The medicine's really working this well? You're not just putting on an act for my benefit?"

"I'd think better than anyone, you'd know my acting isn't much better than my cooking. Why did I hold out for so long against taking this stuff? It's a miracle. For the first time since I've been back on the mountain, I feel like I can do the work necessary to run not just my place, but yours."

"I appreciate that…" She ducked her head in the process, hiding flushed cheeks with a spill of her hair. "But, Wiley, please take this slow. While your pain meds are kicking in, you also need to use that opportunity to do your physical therapy exercises, okay?"

He waved off her concerns. "Stop worrying. I'm a new man, and have you to thank."

Macy prayed the solution to his every problem was this simple.

He didn't just cover her smaller hand but engulfed it. In the process, unlocking a curio cabinet of possibilities. Could a couple pills be all this bear needed to remove the thorn from his paw? Her every instinct screamed for her to be cautious where he was concerned. Nothing this good came easy, but what if it did? What if all the hopes and dreams she'd secretly carried for them just as easily came true?

Of course, she'd lied to her mother.

Macy wasn't just attracted to Wiley, but spellbound. Before tonight, that attraction had been spurred by memories of the guy he used to be, but now that he'd taken his meds, she found it all too easy to focus on the man he was—strong and charming and thoughtful.

When her gaze met his, it became a struggle to even breathe. The intensity that had always drawn her to him was still there. It had been trapped, but was now free—like her.

"How can I ever thank you?" he said.

"You don't have to." Her breath hitched, and she licked her lips. "Helping is what friends do." But the raw truth was that she didn't want to be just his friend. Did that make her a bad person? Helping him, but with a selfish motive?

Was his success with just one round of pain meds still more proof that they were destined to be together? That he was the key to her finding a second chance at love, at life, at *everything*?

They finished eating and took turns feeding Henry his pureed beef and carrots.

They opted to leave kitchen cleanup for later, since Henry had gotten more food in his hair than in his belly, and needed a bath.

Macy drew water in the claw-foot tub that was a twin to the one in Wiley's cabin, then set Henry's plastic bath chair in the center.

Before she'd had a chance, Wiley took Henry from his high chair, and now made funny faces at him in the mirror. She couldn't get over the change. It was truly remarkable. So much so, it was a little scary. The last thing she wanted was to go looking for trouble where there was none, but she couldn't bear to consider what would happen when Wiley's meds wore off.

Would his pain rush back? Or, as long as he kept up his dosage, would it forever be held at bay?

"Isn't that water a little deep for this guy?"

Macy glanced up to find Wiley pointing at the water's rising level.

"Yikes. Thanks. Mind stripping him while I let some out?"

"No problem."

Unlike the bathroom in Wiley's grandfather's cabin, Macy's had been part of a remodel her grandmother had done in the nineties. She'd transformed the second bedroom where her father had grown up into a master bath with double sinks and a wall of windows overlooking the Eagle Ridge valley. She'd moved the antique tub to allow her a beautiful view while soaking up to her neck in bubbles. Where her vanity table had been, Macy now kept Henry's changing table. A vibrant oriental rug covered most of the wood floor, and she'd painted the walls a soothing blue. The golden-hued sunset slanted in deep rays, making the room all the more inviting.

"Here you go, buddy." Wiley slipped Henry into his tub chair. He'd winced, but now that he was on his knees, he took the dolphin mitten sponge from the wire basket hanging over the tub's edge, and squeezed in a dollop of baby shampoo. "I haven't smelled this stuff in years. I guess since I found that stray cat, and Mom made me wash it before letting it in the house. Dollar General had been out of pet shampoo, but they'd had plenty of this."

"I haven't thought about that cat in forever. What did you name her? Tulip? Rose?"

"Daffodil. She ran off not two months after I'd caught her. She always was wild. She's probably still holed up around my parents' old house, terrorizing baby birds and bunnies."

Macy laughed. "Wouldn't surprise me. Seems like ornery pets always live longest, which means Charlie and Lulu should be around a good long while."

Watching Wiley bathe her son did funny things to Macy's stomach—wonderful happy somersaults and flip-flops. He was tender and gentle, yet took time to play with Henry's boats and teach him to splash and make chugging sounds—all the things a father rightfully should. But Wiley wasn't Henry's father, which left Macy all the more confused. How had she come to feel so much for him so fast? Had her sense of failure over the divorce woven its way into her crush on Wiley that had apparently never left her system?

When they knelt shoulder to shoulder, she yearned to lean closer to at least kiss his cheek.

As for kissing his lips?

A hot rush engulfed her. It wasn't as if she was unfamiliar with the birds and bees. So what was it about Wiley that made every slight brush of skin to skin and lingering look such a thrill?

Henry yawned.

Wiley asked, "Getting sleepy, bud?"

"Thanks for your help." Macy reached behind her for her son's giraffe-hooded towel wrap. She stretched it out on the floor, then fished Henry from the tub to plant his behind on the towel before pulling up the hood and wrapping him nice and snug. Bath time was her favorite part of the day. Sharing these precious moments with Wiley made this night all the more special.

She was already carrying Henry to the changing table when she noticed Wiley struggle to get back on his feet. "Need help?"

Lips pressed tight, he shook his head. "I've got this."

He pulled the rubber stopper from the tub, then tucked Henry's toys back in the basket and wrung the dolphin cloth before hanging it over the tub's side.

She kept one eye on him and the other on her son while Wiley used the tub's lip for support. She didn't realize she'd been holding her breath until he stood. Only then, did she dare exhale.

"Maybe you were right about taking it easy," he said with a wry grin.

"What? Could you repeat that?" she teased. "My ears must not be working."

"Watch that sass or I'll flick you with a towel."

"That used to hurt." She finished lotioning Henry and reached for a fresh diaper. "You were so mean."

"Sorry. I was just fooling around. Need help?"

"Sure. Want to grab his pajamas?" She nodded toward

the clothes neatly stacked on the built-in shelves her grandfather had built.

"Will this work?" He handed her a pale blue sleeper patterned with red fire trucks.

"Yep. Thanks."

"I should have driven my truck over. I hate for you to have to get back out now that Henry's ready for bed. How about I walk home? It's a nice night."

"Are you sure you're ready for that? It's only a mile, but still..." She couldn't help but eye him with concern.

"I'll be fine. Tuck your little guy into his crib, and I'll get a jump start on the dishes."

"Don't worry about them," she said. "Cleaning gives me something to do once Henry goes to bed. Then I get to work on my knitting."

"You should be relaxing. Reading or watching TV." As if unsure about his next move, he slipped his hands in his jeans pockets.

"Would you like to help tuck in Henry? I read to him and give him a bottle. He's usually asleep by the end of the book, so the ritual's probably more for me than him, but still..." She smiled. "I enjoy our routine."

"Sounds fun. Thanks."

After fixing the bottle, Macy offered Wiley the nursery's rocker, but he refused, and perched on the cushioned window seat with his legs stretched in front of him.

She had a tough time focusing on *The Lonely Hippo*'s words. The old back porch that her dad had converted into a cozy room was small, and Wiley's large frame seemed to take up half the space.

He paid close attention to the story, almost as if he thought there might be a comprehension test.

When it came time to nestle Henry into his crib, she

noticed Wiley's near reverent touch as he pulled the fuzzy blanket to Henry's shoulders and tucked it in just so.

"He looks content," he noted.

"I know, right? Sometimes I envy his ability to sleep." Her son had already drifted off.

She gathered his empty bottle from the side table next to the rocker, then gestured for Wiley to follow her to the kitchen.

"That was easy enough," Wiley said. "I always gave my folks hell before going to bed."

"Me, too, but remember Henry's only eight months old. Don't jinx me. I've got a long haul till he starts making trouble."

"Aw, he's a sweetheart. With you as a mom, I'll bet it's a sure deal he stays that way."

She started to contradict him, but stopped short of opening her mouth. Whether Wiley's words turned out to be truth or not, for this moment, she'd had her fill of drama and if the future wanted to work out fine, she'd let it. She'd ignore the gnawing at her conscience, the voice telling her there was no way Wiley's turnaround could be real. She'd ignore the other voice reminding her that he was only supposed to be her friend—nothing more. That she wasn't supposed to want to kiss him, or stroke his stubble, or feel his rough fingers strumming her body or explore the possibility of transforming their lifelong friendship into so much more.

"Since my last stab at clearing the table didn't turn out so pretty—" he stood at the kitchen sink, wielding the scrub pad "—how about I do the washing and you handle the legwork?"

"Sounds like a deal."

In less time than she would have liked, dinner was just

a memory save for the stray cracker Blinkie munched beneath the table.

Macy started to say something to break the silence, but Wiley did, too. They both wound up laughing, which, she supposed, was better than a bunch of meaningless babble.

"Guess I should get going while there's still enough light to put up the goat and feed Pancake," he said.

"You decided to keep my silly name?"

He shrugged. "It's as good as any."

She smiled. But then being around him when he was like this made it kind of hard to do anything but wear a cornball grin.

"I can't thank you enough, Mace. Not just for dinner, but well…" He bowed his head. "You know."

Nodding, she stepped forward for a hug.

Being against him was beyond right.

Every inch of their bodies felt as if they'd been made to fit together. An achy, elemental yearning grew inside. More than anything, she wanted to stand on her tiptoes and finally feel his lips against hers as a woman and not a girl. But did he want that, too?

With every part of her being, she hoped so.

For a lingering moment, he tightened his hold, and Macy thought, prayed, wished her kiss was coming. When he grasped her shoulders, holding her just close enough for his warm breath to tickle her upper lip, and then he tilted his head as if contemplating how best to come in for a landing, her heart sang. What else could he be doing but preparing to kiss her?

"Right." He straightened and cleared his throat. "I really need to get going. Blinkie, you coming with me, or staying here?"

The tiny dog skittered to his quilt, curled into a ball, then rested his chin atop his paws.

Wiley laughed. "Guess that answers that. Looks like you have a new dog."

"Oh, no. He can stay for tonight, so you don't have to carry him, but there's no way I can handle two babies in the house."

"Fair enough." He winked. "If we both feel up to it in the morning, want to check some fences? See if we can find a solution to how Charlie's been getting out?"

"Sounds good." Macy tried not to pout. The last thing she wanted was for Wiley to leave. She tried telling herself it was good for him to go. That she needed alone time to process all they'd just been through. But she'd been on her own long enough. She was tired of solitude, and ready to move forward with her downright miraculous second chance.

"Good night." He hesitated, almost as if he planned to say more, but then he left, and Macy struggled to remember what she'd ever done with her nights besides think of him.

## Chapter Ten

Wiley got halfway home when he realized he'd made a mistake.

His meds were wearing off and there wasn't a damned thing he could do about it other than keep putting one foot in front of the other. The farther he went, the more the road unfurled in front of him like an always-extending measuring tape.

He was supposed to take his meds every eight hours, but it had only been four or five. Six, tops. What did that mean for the rest of his night? Should he take more now?

Drink a little, then take more?

Nah, he couldn't do that because Suzy Sunshine poured all his booze down the drain.

What was wrong with him? He'd had an awesome time tonight. The dinner. Henry's bath. Listening to Macy read. At the time, it had all seemed like a fantastical alternative universe. Yet now, he regretted ever having gone. It was no secret she'd wanted to kiss him, and before his accident, he'd have taken full advantage of her female delights. Now? He couldn't.

He'd, of course, remain friendly with her and eat her cooking whenever possible, but sharing more was out of the question. He owed her for convincing him to quit being a stubborn old mule and take his damned pain meds, but that kind of favor needed to be repaid by maybe patching her roof, not kissing her.

By the time he reached his drive, irrational rage pounded along with his head. The unfamiliar exertion had him sweat-covered and out of breath. It was humiliating—how an hour earlier he'd felt on top of the world. Yet now, if he'd been able to bend his knee, he would have crawled.

At the house, the one-eyed cat still sat on the porch rail. She eyed him with suspicion when he took his trusty hoe from the cobwebbed corner.

Wiley made it to the side yard and found the goat still grazing. Considering all the grass had been eaten short, he was lucky the four-legged menace hadn't made it around to the garden.

It had been irresponsible of him to leave him out, but in his defense, Macy had his head spinning. He'd been trapped under water, not knowing which way was up. But then she'd shown him the light and everything changed. He'd broken through the surface and gulped for air and for the few hours he'd been with her and Henry, he could breathe again, and it had been good.

*So good.*

But now he was back under, not sure which way to go.

Leading the goat by his guide rope back to the barn, Wiley considered his options.

Option A: As soon as he finished feeding Pancake and carried the cat in for the night, he could make a run into town for more booze. He could stash it in a place Macy couldn't find and resume the crap life to which he'd grown accustomed.

Option B: Take the meds, and when he had enough relief to do his PT and decent upper body work, take the gamble that given time, his leg function would improve and the pain gradually lessen.

It seemed like a no-brainer. Down a couple pills and be done with it. He was too strong to become a sad statistic.

*Haven't you already become just that by the amount of booze you guzzle damn near every night?*

Wiley ignored the nagging voice in his head, fed Pancake and the goat, locking the goat safely in a pen in the barn for the night. He even managed to wrangle Lulu into the barn. Until she fattened up enough to regain her full strength, she was staying inside at night even though she preferred the pasture. He didn't want to risk coyotes making a meal of her.

Back at the cabin, he took the cat from the rail and headed inside.

She hissed at the intrusion on her solitude.

He hissed back, then set her on the sofa where she jumped onto the back to stare out the window. "Keep it up," he said, "and tomorrow night I'll leave you out for coyote bait."

Of course, he wouldn't, but that was just how pissy he was feeling.

While rummaging for an ice cream sandwich in the freezer, he found vodka Macy had missed. He downed the ice cream in three bites, then fell onto the sofa with the bottle in his hand.

The cat didn't look at him, but she also didn't hiss.

Progress?

Not sure how long he'd be stuck inside when he'd first returned to the mountain, Wiley had signed up for satellite TV, and now switched it on, channel surfing until finding a *River Monsters* rerun.

Reclining, he shoved a few fussy pillows behind his head, then unscrewed the bottle cap and swigged.

It burned good.

"Cat," he said, "I'm sure by now, you feel meds are the

clear way for me to best proceed. But there is a problem." He downed more of the fiery drink. "The pills have a lag time I'm not entirely comfortable with." He waved the bottle in her direction. "Take now, for example. If I follow the directions like a good little patient, I don't think I'm allowed to have a second dose for another hour. Hell, maybe two? It's not like I write this shit down."

Her tail slowly rose up and down. It was a bit snakelike and—not gonna lie—kinda freaked him out.

He drank more.

"So, it's like this. Since I need the meds like every four to five hours, but I'm only allowed to have them every eight hours, what am I supposed to do? Just sit around and suffer during the time in between? Or do I make my own schedule? Take them every six hours? Four hours? Two?"

He toasted the cat with his bottle, then finished it off.

"Good answer." His words were slurred. Or maybe his mind was slurred. Who knew? Who cared?

BANGING ON THE front door woke Wiley.

Sunlight streamed through the windows and instead of sitting all pissed off on the sofa back, the cat sat square in the middle of his chest.

Wiley released a slow exhale. The night seemed to have gotten away from him.

"Good morning," he said to his loyal feline companion. "How come you didn't answer the damned door?" He scooped her up and set her on the floor.

*"Wiley?"* Macy called, her voice muffled from outside. *"I know you're in there!"*

"Coming!" He sat up, only to find that the vodka bottle had also spent the night on his chest. He wedged it between the sofa cushions, for once thankful of the too many pillows his grandfather's lady friends had crocheted, needle-pointed and quilted over the years.

He rolled off the couch, using the coffee table for leverage when he tried and failed under his own steam to get to his feet. He stumbled to the door, unsure how to fake his next steps should Macy want him to go anywhere far.

"Hey." He opened the door, leaning all his weight on it.

"Good morning." She brushed past him, carrying Henry with one arm and Blinkie with the other. "You had me worried. How was your walk home? Did you have much pain?"

"It was all right." *Liar.*

The cat shot out the door and leapt onto the porch rail.

"Have you had your meds yet?"

"No. Just got up."

"You're long past due. Watch these two—" she set Henry and Blinkie on the floor "—I'm grabbing groceries from the truck."

"Aw, Mace, you didn't need to do that."

Midway down the porch stairs, she cast him an over-the-shoulder smile and he was lost. Yes, he'd take the damned meds. For today, for however long she wanted. Might sound corny, but the way she made him feel was better than vodka or any other drug—which had to stop. Time to cool things off before she went and kissed him. She might seem tough as a tanned hide on the outside, but he suspected her divorce had left her a mess inside. As pretty as she was, she'd one day find another guy, but that guy sure as hell couldn't be him.

She deserved way better.

"Need help?" he asked more from a sense of duty than because he might have actually been helpful.

"No, thanks. I only have a few bags."

He yawned. "What time is it that you've already been to town and back?"

"Ten." Her glare told him he should have been up earlier. But why? Without her here, there wasn't much beyond feeding the pets that he cared to do. "I'll bet you haven't eaten yet, either?"

"Not unless the cat fed me a breakfast burrito in my sleep." He scratched his chest.

She scowled. "Wiley… I thought last night you agreed to let me help you? But nothing I do will change your life for the better if you refuse to help yourself."

He decided to be honest. "Right now, I'm hurting, okay? The pain makes it hard to think—or even see straight. Give me a sec, and I'll get with the program."

"Sit. I'll fix you eggs and toast so you can take your medicine. Then we'll establish a physical therapy schedule."

"How about you slow down?" He did sit, but on a counter bar stool so he didn't have to bend his leg.

"Not going to happen." She unloaded eggs and cheese and milk and butter into his fridge at a frenetic pace. Then came bread and graham crackers and peanut butter that she stashed in the same cabinet his grandfather had. It felt good that she remembered. As if a piece of his grandpa lived on outside his memory. "After last night, I expected to find you already getting a jump start on your day. You did take your medicine last night, didn't you? It works better if you take it regularly as prescribed."

"You sound like a walking drug commercial."

"Sorry, I'm not sorry. Grandma broke her hip a few years back, and I was in charge of her care. I'm just repeating what her doctor told me."

"Lay off. I'll take the damn medicine." Wiley leaned on the counter, covering his face with his hands.

"Why didn't you take it last night?"

"Because I passed out drunk and forgot, okay?" He

hadn't meant to snap, but sometimes the woman went too far. She acted as though they were already a couple, but they weren't—would never be. The sooner she figured that out, the better off he'd be.

Hands on her hips, mouth puckered into a frown, she didn't say anything, just stood there shaking her head. Her body language told him what he already knew. He was a total screwup. Jackass. Lazy son of a bitch. He hated himself. Moreover, hated seeing his shortcomings reflected in her beautiful eyes.

"I'll take the damned meds, okay? I slipped. I found the vodka in the freezer, and thought I'd have a few sips, but my leg was hurting so freakin' bad, I wasn't sure if I could even leave the sofa to find my pills. As far as I know, that was the last of my booze."

"You won't buy more?"

He shook his head.

Blinkie yapped at his feet.

Wiley looked down to find that Henry had crawled after him. The tiny baby and even smaller dog made quite a pair. In ways, they reminded Wiley of Macy and him. He just sat there, feeling like a big baby while she yapped away.

She wadded the grocery bag she'd just unloaded. "How do I know I can trust you?"

"You don't." He hung his head. And that was the truth of it. She and Doc could try all the homespun cures in the world to save him, but what if he was already too far gone? He didn't want to believe that, but he'd been trained to deal in concrete facts and his current MO was shaded in nothing but fuzzy gray.

She abandoned her high ground on the opposite side of the island counter to hug him from behind. He closed his eyes, welcoming her heat. He didn't deserve her, but he wanted her. He could ask himself how he'd let her become so important in such a short period of time, but that would be stupid. He may have been gone from this mountain, but she'd never left his soul. She'd been right there all the time.

Something tugged the leg of his jeans. Wiley looked down to find Henry pulling himself up. Was that normal? "Mace, hate to interrupt this riveting episode of *All About Me*, but look at your kid."

Macy shrieked. "Henry! You pulled yourself up! You're starting to walk." To Wiley, she said, "Don't move a muscle, I have to take a pic for his scrapbook or Mom will have my hide."

What a privilege to catch Henry pulling himself up for the first time. The kid's father was missing that milestone in his son's life, but Wiley had a front row seat. What other firsts might he be fortunate enough to witness if surrendering to the meds brought him enough solace to lay off the booze? Knowing the uphill battle his friends' faced fighting pain-med addictions—some had been in drug addiction treatment longer than physical therapy—Wiley was beyond wary to climb on board the medication train, but what could it hurt to at least take them as prescribed for a week and then reassess his situation?

MACY DIDN'T TAKE one picture, but a dozen, then promptly texted them to her mom and Wendy. She next made Wiley a cheese omelet and toast. He took his meds with a nice big glass of OJ, and thirty minutes later became a new man, searching for a way to take Henry and Blinkie on their trek to mend fences.

"Got it." Wiley dashed toward the bedroom.

If she hadn't witnessed his transformation with her own eyes, she wouldn't have believed it. When the medicine gave him this much relief, why hadn't he taken it on his own? What was she missing?

He returned, waving a faded red backpack. "Looks like I found Blinkie's ride."

"I don't think he's going to like being crammed into that musty old thing."

"He will by the time I'm done with it." He fished through a junk drawer for scissors, then cut a bunch of windows, and a skylight at the top. "Taa freakin' daa."

"Hate to admit it, but that's pretty cool. Have an old towel to put in the bottom?"

He laughed. "This place has nothing but old towels."

"Since you're being utilized for more important things, I'll find the towel." Henry had crawled to Wiley and now used him again for support, grinning at the cleverness of his new trick.

"Hey, buddy. You look like future SEAL material."

*"Agggghhhhh! Eeee!"* Henry danced his soft baby boots atop Wiley's bare feet.

The sight of her tiny baby with the great big cowboy ruined any resolve Macy might have had to be cautious with her heart. Raising Henry without a father was hard, but her added workload had never been the main issue. Most of all, she hated knowing he'd miss out on all the special times he could have shared with his dad. Of course, she was being ridiculously premature, but what if Wiley kept improving? What if he eventually grew strong enough to view her as more than a temporary wellness coach?

"Look at him go," Wiley said. "He's amazing."

Hope rose as surely in her chest as a holiday balloon, but then it burst when sanity returned. What was wrong with her? Spinning fairy tales about living happily ever after with the boy next door when there was nothing happy about either of their stories. Allowing herself to be even temporarily swept into a fantasy of the two of them being together was a fool's game. She'd already been cheated on by one man she'd loved.

Who was to say that once Wiley regained his health, he wouldn't morph right back into the ladies' man he'd once been? Back in school, he hadn't had a few girlfriends, but an entire stable. What made Macy think she was anyone special?

"You have an awesome kid."

"Thank you." Needing distance to get her head back in the right place to spend all day working alongside Wiley, Macy asked, "We could be out a while. Should I pack a few sandwiches?"

"I guess. But nothing too fancy. You know I hate picnics." He lifted Henry into his arms, then headed to the back of the cabin before returning a few minutes later.

"Where'd you go?"

He brandished his pain meds. "Just in case."

"We won't be gone that long, will we? You won't need to take it again until six tonight."

"That's why I said, *just in case*. It's not a big deal."

But to Macy, it was. It meant a lot that he was thinking ahead. That implied planning and responsibility. It told her he cared about getting better, which was a very good thing. As for his disliking picnics, of course, she remembered. But maybe she could be the one to show him that when you shared them with the right person, they could be an awful lot of fun.

Could Macy tell what he was up to?

They'd been walking their shared fence line for three hours, making needed repairs along the way, and had just stopped for their meal. While she changed Henry's diaper, Wiley downed two more pills with bottled water—not a good sign. This was the very reason he'd fought taking them. They made it all too easy to pretend his strength had fully returned.

Maintaining that illusion was costly.

Keeping it together at the cabin that morning had been a struggle when she'd questioned him on why he was bringing the entire bottle. How did he explain the terror he'd felt when the drug's freeing effect had worn off?

As if one minute he'd stood at the edge of a cliff, and the next, been shoved off. He wasn't going through that again.

From now on, even though the dosage said to take two pills every eight hours, he'd take them every six—except when he was sleeping.

He may be jumping the gun on this latest dose, but the physical labor was hell not just on his leg, but back and shoulders. After a few weeks of a daily work routine, he'd no doubt feel great. Until then, he'd use the pills as a crutch. Knowing he had time before becoming addicted made him all the more convinced this was a good idea. Once he regained his strength, he'd no longer even need meds.

"There you go," Macy said in a singsong voice to her son. "You're all nice and clean."

The baby giggled.

"That's got to be the best sound on earth," Wiley noted. "It's pretty infectious."

They loaded the dog and child back into their respective carriers, then continued down the fence line. The going was rough—not just the rocky terrain, heavily forested with ponderosa pine and Douglas fir, but forging their way through thick undergrowth of elk sedge, creeping Oregon grape and bitterbrush.

Beneath slanted sunbeams, they walked in companionable silence for a mile, stopping to straighten leaning posts or restring wire where branches had fallen. Odds

were, they'd already patched Charlie's escape route closer
to Wiley's cabin.

"How long do you think it's been since anyone's been
up here?" They'd stopped at an old campsite and found
blackened rocks from a fire ring and a bunch of rusty tin
cans. A few lantern hooks had grown into the trees.

"I'd say at least forty years. Maybe not since Clem and
Buster constructed it." Wiley used his shirt sleeve to wipe
sweat from his forehead.

"Do you think our grandmothers went with them? You
know, to make an outing of the chore?"

He laughed. "I think you're romanticizing what must
have been a helluva lot of backbreaking work. Think about
it. They had to haul all the supplies and tools, cut the posts
as they went along, as well as dig the holes. Meanwhile
our grandmothers were probably stuck inside, canning."

"Tell me about your grandmother."

"I don't know much." He used a hammer to pound in
one of the staples that held the wire in place. The feed store
carried handheld staple drivers, but he didn't mind doing
the job the way his grandfather would have. "Sylvia died
when I was five. Grandpa dated a bunch, but never did
remarry. She was a teacher—moved here from Chicago
when she was fresh out of college. They met at a Memo-
rial Day town picnic, fell in love and never looked back.
Dad said her family was none too happy to have their
fine, educated daughter end up with a mountain man, but
they eventually got over it. By the time my dad was born,
they'd even come out for visits. She was the first teacher
at what's now the abandoned mountain school."

"Did you ever meet them—your great-grandparents?"

"Nah. Everyone in my family has a nasty habit of dying
young. Not sure why I'm even still alive."

"Wiley James." Her glare was none too happy. "That's a horrible thing to say."

"Why? I'm not looking for sympathy, but genuinely curious. Why am I still here when my life feels pretty hopeless?"

"I once asked the same thing. Rex had just left me. My baby bump was too big for me to see my feet, and I didn't see the point of anything—except every so often, this little guy—" she jiggled Henry's feet "—would kick. I took his every movement as a sign. Like the universe's way of waving to get my attention. Sure, my life might have sucked back then, but not to the degree that I'd ever seriously considered checking out. Is that how you feel? Suicidal?"

He shook his head. "Forget I said anything."

"Now, you've got me genuinely concerned."

"Don't be."

"If you're looking for a reason to live, think how much your pets need you."

He laughed. "Aside from Blinkie, that crew's on autopilot."

"Okay…" From behind him, she sucked in a swift breath. "What if I confessed that I need you?"

"Is this a hypothetical confession or the real deal?"

"What if it is real? Maybe I do need you. Would that be so bad?"

He froze, then turned to clamp his hands over her shoulders. "For you, that wouldn't just be bad, but a full-on Texas twister of a disaster. Thought we'd already been over this?"

*"We have."* She raised her chin. "But what if I think the issue needs revisiting?"

"I'd tell you you're about three peaches shy of a bushel."

He left her to keep walking. Facing her hadn't been good for his system. His pulse had gone haywire and his mouth dry. Being close to her was bad for business—especially when his business consisted solely of maintaining status quo. He needed more attachments as much as he needed another cluster bomb to his remaining good leg.

"Know what I think?" She passed on his right, giving him too good a view of her amazing behind and little Henry giggling and pointing at yapping Blinkie.

"Don't care," he said over the obnoxious dog.

"I think you're chicken," she said, swiveling to face him.

He snorted. "I think if you don't stop walking backward, you're gonna fall."

"You'll catch me."

"Nope."

Sure enough, she tripped. If it hadn't been for Henry, Wiley might have let her go down to teach her a lesson, but no way would he risk the baby being hurt on his watch. His reflexes were sluggish on the meds, but his hands connected with her waist in time to pull her up against him.

"You're welcome," he said with his mouth an inch from hers.

"Told you you'd catch me."

"I only did it because of your son."

"Uh-huh…"

Her smile brought on a heat wave that had nothing to do with the day's waning sun.

"I think there's a part of you, Wiley James, who, to this very day, still wonders what might've happened had my dad not interrupted."

# Chapter Eleven

"Woman—" Wiley released her to keep right on walking "—stop talking crazy and get moving. Otherwise, we'll never get this menagerie back to the cabin by sunset."

"Whatever. I still say you're chicken." Macy could razz Wiley all she wanted, but deep down, she was the one who'd been curious all these years.

"I say your sassy mouth shouldn't be writing checks your body can't cash."

"Whoa—do you mean can't or *won't*? There's a big difference." He'd picked up the pace, and she had a devil of a time keeping up. His meds must be working overtime. "In your case, I think we'd be dealing with the latter."

He answered with an indecipherable grunt.

It was another thirty minutes before they reached the corner where their grandparents' shared property boundary ended, and national forest land began.

"Let's call it a day," she suggested. "We'll start here when we have more time."

"Agreed. Besides, I doubt even Charlie would make it this far from the pasture."

It took another hour to reach Macy's cabin, and Henry cried the whole way.

Charlie spit at Wiley as he passed.

The lady llamas ignored them to keep right on grazing.

Because of the shape of their grandparents' land parcels, their pastures ran side by side.

As if curious about the commotion, Lulu stood near her side of the fence.

"What's wrong with Henry?" Wiley called above the wails.

"My guess is that he's tired and has spent far too long in his carrier. Let me get all of us fed, and then we can walk back to your place for my truck."

"I'll get it." He shrugged off his pack. "Give me your keys, and take the dog."

"Are you sure?" She took Blinkie out for a cuddle. "This adventure has to have been rough on your leg, and it's past time for your second round of meds."

With a jangle of her keys in the otherwise still night air, he waved off her concern. "I'll take it when I get back."

Once he'd gone, she set Blinkie on the porch, then took off Henry's carrier. He was still huffy and his poor eyes were red-rimmed and shiny with tears.

"I'm sorry." She carried him inside, holding open the door for the dog to follow.

Blinkie remembered where she'd set his water dish and took a good, long drink.

She deposited Charlie in his high chair, wet a rag at the sink to wash his chubby hands and face, then handed him a teething biscuit and the dog some plain yogurt.

Now, what should she make for the grown-ups?

After perusing her pantry, she settled on mac and cheese and salads. There was some venison sausage her dad made in the freezer, so she popped that in the microwave to thaw, then fed Henry pureed pears, pork and green beans. Tonight's grown-up dinner might be too tough on his tummy. Some table foods made him irritable, so she'd been hold-

ing back until his nine-month wellness check, which was
only a week away.

By the time truck headlights reflected in the kitchen
window, dinner was done. Macy sat at the table in the chair
beside her son, balling yarn.

"I was getting worried," she said when Wiley strode
through the front door.

Blinkie barked, as if defending his home.

"I had to feed everyone and put the horse and goat in
the barn for the night—which reminds me, I still need to
ask Doc if he knows of anyone wanting to sell a few goat
companions."

"Want to use my phone?"

"Nah. It can wait till morning." He eyed the set table
and still-steaming entrées. "This looks great. Thanks for
cooking."

"You're welcome. Thanks for getting my truck."

"My pleasure." His gallant nod was swoon worthy. All
day, she'd fought her physical attraction. His painkillers
truly must be remarkable for him to be already back on
top of his game.

"How's your leg? Take your medicine?"

"Yes, ma'am." He sat in the chair across from her.
"Mind if I dig in?"

"Please do." Her chest swelled with unexpected emotion. The normalcy of this scene was almost too much to
bear. When Rex left, she'd feared her life would never be
normal again. Might be old-fashioned, but she'd adored
being married. She'd enjoyed the comforting routines, and
knowing if she heard a bump in the night she had big,
strong arms to reassure her everything would be fine.

Trouble was, her wedded bliss with Rex had been all
one-sided. If she and Wiley did connect, would he love her
as much as she suspected she'd be capable of loving him?

At first, Wiley ate with gusto, but then slowed. His movements grew sluggish, as if operating underwater.

"Are you okay?" she asked when he almost spilled the glass of iced tea she'd set next to his plate.

"*Perrrfect.* Is it just me, or does it seem like we have a real nice family vibe going?"

"It sure does." Even though his slurred speech guaranteed the drugs were talking and not he, Macy didn't care. She'd much rather see Wiley a little loopy than in pain.

"If I'd come back to this mountain before screwing up my leg, I might have put moves on you, Miss Macy."

Her pulse galloped. "Oh?"

"Shoot, I used to call my granddad every Sunday when I wasn't overseas. Well, sometimes even then, but when you can't find a phone, it can be surprisingly tough making a call." He winked.

Macy knew this was hardly the time to focus on his kissable lips, or the way she craved touching his stubble, but she couldn't help wondering if she would be a bad person by using his mellow mood to her advantage?

"So anyway, I was in Afghanistan—maybe Syria—and it was hot as balls, but I was talking to Granddad, and he told me to get home, because you were about to marry some damn fool, and the only one who could stop you from making the biggest mistake of your life was me."

"Wait—Buster really said all of that?"

He crossed his heart. "If I'm lyin', I'm dyin'…" There he went again with his wink. "Granddad pushed you like a drug until even I started thinking maybe we might at least hook up."

*Hook up?* She'd been hoping for something a little more romantic, but it was at least a start.

*A start to what?* her grown-up conscience fairly

screamed. *This man is trouble with a capital* T*!* Her giddy teenaged heart didn't care.

"How long has it been since you got any?"

She gulped, then coughed, then tried saving face by downing half her tea. "*Any*, as in…"

"S-E-X," he whispered. "I'm spelling it in case little ears are listening."

"Yeah, pretty sure Henry doesn't know what that means." But she did! And judging by the swift hum between her legs, her body felt it had been way too long since she'd last fooled around.

"Well?" He crossed his arms, fixing her with a direct stare as if fully expecting an answer.

"Obviously—" she ducked to avoid having him see the raging inferno playing out on her cheeks "—my last time was with my husband."

"He probably wasn't as good as me."

She choked on her latest sip of tea. "*Wiley!* Stop."

"Oh, I'm just getting started, little lady. This afternoon, you called me a chicken, but tonight, I'm going to show you…" He leaned toward her, but seemed confused when he couldn't quite bridge the last three feet. "Whoa…"

"I think you should rev those engines of yours right onto my sofa and sleep it off. Your meds are making you say things that, come morning, you'll regret." She stood to clear the table.

"The only thing I regret is not coming back to the mountain early enough to save you from Evil Rex." When she reached for his plate, he pulled her onto his lap, holding her tight while she struggled to remember how to breathe. She desperately wanted anything he had to give her, but not like this.

He should be sober, and in full command of his faculties, and—

He cut off her thoughts by coming closer, *closer*, and then, just when she feared dying from anticipation, he finally, *finally* pressed his lips to hers.

She closed her eyes and sighed.

Was this really happening?

Was he increasing his pressure and slipping her his tongue? And was she all-in, kissing him right here at her grandparents' kitchen table, right in front of her son?

Thinking of Henry had Macy pulling away, and scrambling to her feet.

"Come back…" Wiley's sexy-slow grin made her almost wish for a second she wasn't a mom, so she could focus on being a woman.

"I can't. I—I have things to do." Things like clearing the table and bathing her son and putting him to bed, when what she'd rather be doing was taking unfair advantage of her clearly inebriated guest.

*"Noooo,"* he whined. "Wouldn't you rather *do* me?"

"That's it…" She helped him to his feet. Additional touching did little to help maintain her resolve, especially when he accidentally grazed her ultrasensitive breasts. "How about you wait for me on the sofa?"

"Sounds like a plan." He winked.

When she'd assisted him into the living room, she next made quick work of getting him stretched out with his head propped on a couple throw pillows. She removed his boots, then covered him with one of her grandmother's afghans. But that wasn't enough to warm his entire body, so she had to take the one off the back of her grandfather's recliner, too.

"Wait," Wiley said when she returned to the kitchen to get Henry for his bath. "Aren't you joining me?"

"Absolutely," she lied. "Stay there, and I'll be back with a surprise."

*"Oooooh..."* His brown eyes widened. "I like surprises. I'll be right here."

Macy bathed Henry, read him a story and tucked him in for the night. She cleared the table and washed their few dishes and slipped the leftovers into the fridge.

And all the while, Wiley remained on the sofa—snoring.

She sat in Clem's recliner to take it all in. So much had happened, yet really, nothing at all.

If she closed her eyes, she could still feel the tickle of Wiley's whiskers against her chin. The searing heat of his body against hers. She wanted to cherish that moment and keep it tucked inside her heart, but what was the point? Wiley hadn't kissed her out of any overwhelming, undeniable sense of attraction, but because he'd been high on pain meds.

Hadn't she spent enough time with a man who didn't want her? She could spin all the fantasies she wanted of her and Wiley becoming an official couple, but she wasn't willing to settle for less than real love.

"You're back..."

Macy looked up to find Wiley staring. A faint smile curved his lips at the corners. He needed a shave and his hair needed cutting, yet somehow he still managed to be just as handsome as the teen she'd crushed on so many years ago.

"I figured you'd gone to bed."

"I'm on my way." She rested her clammy palms atop her thighs.

"About earlier—sorry. I didn't mean to manhandle you. Kissing seemed like a great idea at the time, but the last thing I want is to give you the wrong impression."

What did that mean? Did he regret kissing her? His apology was so unexpected, all she could do was stare.

"You're my friend, you know? And right about now, I don't have many."

She cleared her throat. "You probably have more than you know if you'd just let them in."

"Moot point, considering at the moment, all I want is you."

"You mean in a platonic way? As in, you want for us to keep being friends?" *What if I want more? What if I think you're denying your attraction to me? The true depth of your feelings?*

"Yeah, Mace…" He rose onto his elbow. "I do want us to always be friends. What you did for me in getting me to stop drinking and start taking the pills my doctor prescribed was life changing. With that medicine, I'm going to get back in shape and get everything on both of our places returned to perfect working order. I've got big plans—for you, too, if you're amenable."

She leaned forward, wishing her pulse would slow. "I'm listening."

"Hear me out—I know this is going to sound crazy, but—"

Her heart pounded, unsure where he was heading.

"What if I got a few more horses, and started a trail riding business? You could do the cooking for old-fashioned chuck wagon dinners. Tourists would literally eat that up."

"Wait—what?"

"Today's hike gave me a lot of time to think. This mountain is beautiful, but tough to see on foot. You know ever since I got food poisoning my junior year at the field day picnic that I've hated picnics of any kind, but today turned out to be fun. I just thought the two of us could turn that into a nice sum of extra cash."

"No."

"But wait, you haven't heard—"

"I don't want to go into business with you. I deserve more."

His pinched expression read puzzled. "Okay… What do you want?"

She forced a deep breath. "Marry me."

"W-what?" He suffered a coughing spell. "Mace, that's crazy. And considering some of the nutty stuff I spew while I'm on my meds, I should know. I'm the last guy in the world you should want to be with."

"Think about it." She knelt alongside the couch to hold out her hands to him. "On our own, we're each a mess. But together…" Cheeks flushed, though common sense told her to shut up, her mouth kept right on justifying her proposal that had been just plain silly on every level except for deep in her lonely heart. "I know you don't love me, and I don't love you— Well, I always have, but it's been a warm and fuzzy love. You were one of my best friends. But what if that friendship grew into more? I'm lonely, and you need help getting back on your feet. If you wanted to start a business, we could do that. Most of all, I just want to be with you. Look how much we've accomplished in a couple days. Imagine what we could do given a shared lifetime?"

"Mace…" He refused to meet her gaze, but squeezed her hands. "Think about what you're saying. You don't really want to marry me after two good days. It's been years since we were together. You don't even know me, and I sure don't know you."

"Bull." She was already in this deep. Why not dive all the way under? "I can't remember a time when you weren't in my life. Even when you were overseas, I prayed for your safety every night." She reached for the Bible that she kept on the coffee table, and removed the worn photo she'd kept inside. It was of Wiley, looking more handsome than any man had a right to in his Navy dress whites. "Look, I even had this to remind me of our connection."

"Buster gave this to you? Why?" Hands trembling, he took the image from her.

"Honestly? I think you know that answer as well as I do. He wanted me to bring you home." Her voice cracked. "I hate what you went through to get back to this mountain, but now that you're here, I can't fathom letting you go."

"You don't mean that. Hooking up with me will bring you nothing but pain."

"You're wrong." She swallowed the knot in her throat. This wasn't like her to beg, but she so badly wanted her second chance at love that desperation clung to her like a stubborn vine. With all her heart, she believed Wiley was her official second chance. Henry's second chance to have a real father. "At least promise you'll think about it?"

"No." Steely determination hardened his jaw.

"Why not?" He tried escaping her, but apparently her hold was too strong—both figuratively and literally. If he'd just surrender, he'd see. Her belief in their fairy tale was strong enough to carry both of them into their shared future.

He didn't answer.

"I asked you a question…" She leaned in close enough to kiss him, confident that he was infinitely more sober than their last go-round. His warm breath teased her lips. She wanted him so bad, the longing had become a physical ache.

Low in her belly, attraction balled into a wicked, wanton thing. Her every womanly instinct told her he wanted this, too.

"I know this pouty look…" He cupped his hand to her cheek, sweeping her jawline with his thumb. Erotic tingles made it impossible to think. "You used it on your grandparents every time you wanted something from a new doll to that palomino. But what you want from me now makes no sense—for either of us. Tell me you understand…"

She tried looking away, but his stare's magnetic pull was too strong.

He moved his thumb to her lower lip, stroking, transferring his heat, his essence into every inch of her lonely body.

When he bowed his head, angling just so before pressing the sweetest, softest, most mind-numbingly erotic kiss to her lips, her limbs turned weak. "You taste just as good as you did the last time we tried this."

She joined him on the sofa, and when he inched her closer, the size of his erection confirmed his attraction.

Wiley grinned. "Your dad's not lurking in a closet, is he?"

"Hope not." She returned his kiss with one of her own.

"What are we doing?" he asked, pressing his lips to hers again and again.

"Only what we should have been doing years ago." In a bold move, she unbuttoned his fly.

"Mace, hold up. Let's think about this. I don't even have protection."

"I don't care." She angled him back to the sofa, kissing the whole way with the dog nipping at their feet.

"Hush," he said to Blinkie.

The dog increased his volume.

Macy gave her cowboy a light shove to the seat cushions. When he was all the way down, she straddled him, wishing she'd changed into a dress for dinner, so there'd now be fewer clothes.

Blinkie turned frantic, tearing at the sofa skirt with short growls.

"I'm sorry," Wiley said after one more kiss, "but this

isn't working. The yapping dog. The setting. Our first time should be special." He shifted her off of him to cradle his forehead in his hands.

She sat back, blinking past his rejection's sting. "So then you've thought about it? The two of us..." Her blazing cheeks finished the sentence.

"Damn right. But in all my raunchy fantasies, there was never a three-legged dog hell-bent on stopping us."

Up from the couch, he glared at the now quiet dog. "Thanks again for dinner. Talk to you in the morning?"

"Sure." Cross-legged, Macy strove for a casual pose that showed she was cool with all that had transpired, when nothing could be further from the truth. "But you can stay—if you want."

"Thanks, but it's probably best I head home."

"I meant it," she blurted.

"That you want to marry me?" He froze. A myriad of emotions played across his features. There was physical pain in his drawn mouth and maybe anger in his narrowed gaze. Was it her he was upset with? Or the cards he'd been dealt?

Regardless, it might be summer, but sanity crashed into her with an avalanche's icy rush. What was she doing? Asking Wiley to marry her had been stupid. He wasn't the second chance she so desperately craved, but a full-on disaster. "Look, when I suggested we marry, I don't know what I was thinking. At the time, it seemed like a great idea, but—"

"But now, you wish you'd never asked, and I'd just go?"

She winced. "Yes. You were right. It was a horrible idea—for too many reasons to count." But if that were true, why did her heart feel as if it were breaking?

*Because truth hurts.*

She thought about what had happened—first Wiley's

behavior was erratic from too much drinking, then he took meds and tonight, had an even crazier spell when he'd kissed her. Once and for all, for her sake, for Henry's, Macy needed to banish Wiley from her system.

They would always be friends, but never anything more.

# Chapter Twelve

"Thanks for bringing this guy some company," Wiley said to Doc Carthage. Despite the day's drizzle, Wiley's goat and three new lady friends made themselves at home in the front yard. Lulu stood at the pasture gate, checking out the latest action. Wiley was glad for the distraction as it had been a week since Macy proposed, then reneged, and aside from basic pleasantries, she hadn't talked to him since.

"No problem." The vet raised the tailgate on his truck. "Just keep an eye on our pal Charlie, over there." He nodded toward the fence separating Wiley's property from Macy's. Charlie and his angels stood in a row, watching the proceedings. "He might take on a protector role with the goats."

"Is that safe? Charlie's a big boy."

"Should be beneficial unless Charlie decides to get frisky with one of your nannies. He might take a liking to Lulu, too."

"I just got all the fences in good shape, so hopefully, that won't be a problem."

"Good to know." Doc Carthage rounded the side of his truck to climb behind the wheel. "I see the cat up on your porch, but where's Blinkie?"

"Macy's son got such a kick out of the little guy that she kept him."

"Well, that didn't go as planned."

"How so?" Wiley leaned on the truck's hood.

"I thought Macy would get one look at you with that heartbreaker of a dog and rescue the both of you. Never thought she'd keep the mutt and dump you."

"We were hardly an item."

"That won't stop an old man from trying. That girl's carried a torch for you since she was old enough to chase you, so what's the problem?"

*I'm an ass.*

"Two healthy kids like yourselves should be well on your way to making magic happen." He winked. "Fourth of July is right around the corner. Why not invite her to the town picnic? My wife's on the planning committee and there's gonna be plenty of good food and music— fireworks at the high school football stadium once the sun goes down."

"Sounds nice, but I'm not really a picnic kind of guy."

"That's a bunch of bullarky. See you there."

With Doc Carthage gone, Wiley worked in the garden until he could no longer stand the pain, and then he took more pills and sat on the porch with the cat until the medicine kicked in. He'd abandoned any set dosage schedule. It made more sense to take it as needed.

As his prescription was running low, he'd started drinking again at night—just to conserve the meds that made it possible for him to live a mostly normal life during the day.

Since he'd worked up a tolerance, he no longer experienced the mega-highs he'd had when first starting the drug. He did his physical therapy exercises as directed, and had even set up a simple strength-building routine he followed each morning in the barn after feeding Pancake her breakfast.

He'd even thought about saddling Lulu, but she still

hadn't gained enough weight that he felt right about riding her. Soon, though.

Things were, for once, going good.

So why wasn't it enough? Why couldn't he get that last night with Macy from his mind? Their first kiss had been everything he'd thought it would be in a hundred different daydreams, but that didn't give him the right to screw up her life—which he'd surely do if they took things much further.

As for her marriage proposal?

He still didn't get it. What did she see in him? Because from where he was standing, he didn't find himself to be all that great a catch.

So why was his stomach knotted with regret? Why did he crave not only her cooking, but more kisses and the mere pleasure of watching her or little Henry smile?

Trying to put her out of his mind, Wiley called in his prescription to be refilled, then drove into town. He would have liked to grab a coffee, but didn't care to risk tangling with Macy's friend.

He made a quick liquor store run, then sat in the pharmacy's drive-through, only to learn the window was broken, and he'd have to park and go in.

He darted around an elderly woman who was stocking up on patriotic paper plates and napkins only to run into the last people he wanted to see—Macy's mom, Macy and Henry.

"Wiley James? Is that you?"

"Yes, ma'am. Good to see you, Mrs. Shelton." He extended his hand to Macy's mother to shake. It didn't escape him that her daughter refused to even look his way.

Mrs. Shelton made a face. "Put your hand down and give me a proper hug."

He gave her a quick embrace.

Henry squirmed to be next for Wiley's attention.

"Hey, buddy." Wiley tweaked the infant's sneaker-covered foot.

Henry held out his arms as if he wanted Wiley to hold him.

A bark erupted from Macy's purse. Blinkie poked his head out of the top.

"Hush," she said to the dog.

Wiley couldn't help but crack a smile, but then he caught sight of Macy's frown and sobered. How had their friendship gone so wrong, so fast? She hadn't been serious about marrying, had she?

"Macy," her mom said, "I told you to park in the shade and leave that dog in the car."

"I couldn't do that. He's too tiny."

Her mother shook her head.

"Mom, come on. I have to get Henry to the doctor in twenty minutes."

"What's wrong with him?" Wiley asked, surprised by how much he genuinely cared.

"Nothing." The chill in Macy's tone was enough to have him needing a jacket. "He needs his nine-month checkup."

"Good." His shoulders sagged in relief. *I've missed you,* he wanted to say. *I'd forgotten the way sunshine sparks off the blond in your hair.* "I'm glad he's okay."

"You look great." Macy's mother eyed him up and down. "Yes, sir, you're a cool drink of water."

*"Mom!"* Macy gave her mom a swat.

"What? He's a fine-looking young man. I might be married, but I'm not dead."

Macy rolled her eyes, hoisting Henry higher on her hip. "We really need to go."

"All right. But let me grab my tableware."

"It was good seeing you, Mrs. Shelton." Wiley gave her another hug.

"Good seeing you, sweetie. In fact, how about if you stop by for the Fourth of July? Macy's daddy is roasting a pig, so we'll eat all afternoon, and then walk down to the high school for fireworks. Sound good?"

"I appreciate the offer, but…"

"Mom, I'm sure Wiley's busy. Aren't you?" The dirty look Macy shot told him he'd better turn down her mother's offer, or else. But what if he wanted to spend another day with Macy and her son? Not mending fences or pulling weeds in their gardens, but getting to know each other all over again the way they should have from the start.

"Aw, Wiley, please say you'll come. Steve and I would love to have you."

Macy damn near set him on fire with the heat of her angry stare.

"Thank you for the invitation," he said, smiling in Macy's direction. "I would be honored to come. Anything I need to bring?"

"Just your handsome self."

ONCE THE DOCTOR gave Henry a clean bill of health, Macy drove straight to Wiley's, grumbling all the way.

"He's got some nerve," she said to her son just past the abandoned schoolhouse. The sight reminded her of the sweet story about Wiley's great-grandmother. Bet she wouldn't have put up with his bad manners. Most men who had just turned down a marriage proposal wouldn't have the gall to then practically invite themselves to a family picnic! And Wiley hated picnics!

Henry ignored her to chew his plastic key chain.

Blinkie had fallen asleep.

"You two are zero help."

Twenty minutes later, she pulled into Wiley's drive.

He emerged from the barn with Pancake trailing after him. Four rambunctious puppies tumbled ahead.

Macy's fiery temper cooled—a little. But just because he had adorable dogs didn't let him off her hook. The second she killed the engine, she hopped out of the truck.

"There's no way you're coming to Mom's party."

"Nice to see you, too." He wielded that damned sexy grin like a weapon that cut right through her. Why did he have to choose now to be charming? And handsome! He wore his beaten straw cowboy hat disgustingly well, and his faded jeans hugged every inch of his perfect rear. His medicine had transformed him. Gone was the man she'd known who'd been downright hateful due to pain. He'd been replaced by this new and improved version she had no idea how to handle.

"I mean it," she said. "It's going to be tough enough to sit through an endless day of family fun on my own. Doing it with you beside me would be impossible."

"Why?"

"As if you don't know?" A near hysterical laugh passed her lips as she took Henry and Blinkie from the truck.

"You and I both know I'm no good for you."

"Then why come to a family party?"

"Because I was invited?"

Henry wriggled and held out his arms to the enemy.

"Can I hold him?" Wiley asked.

She should have refused, but that would only hurt her son who was clearly a traitor, so she passed Henry to Wiley.

"Hey, buddy." The cowboy tickled her son's belly.

Henry giggled.

"How'd you get so much bigger in a week?"

Blinkie barked at Wiley's feet, demanding his share of attention.

Macy picked up the dog. "Back to the topic at hand, what's it going to take for you to skip the Fourth of July picnic?"

"More than you've got to offer. I think it sounds fun."

"No, you don't. You hate picnics."

"I might have changed my mind."

"You already went on one the day we checked fences, and you didn't seem to have a whole lot of fun."

To Henry, Wiley said, "Do you hear how your mommy's talking to me? Is she always this salty?"

Her traitor son blew a raspberry and giggled.

Blinkie wriggled in her arms as if he wanted in on the action. She put him down.

"In fact," she said, "seems to me, I tried making it more enjoyable, and you rejected my offer. I called you chicken, and even then you wouldn't touch me. How do you think that made me feel? And then, once we got back to the house and we did pick up where we left off all those years ago, and it was every bit as amazing as I'd dreamed, you rejected me again." Her voice cracked. "You destroyed me, Wiley—and not for the first or even second time, but for more times than I can even count. I've tried needling you and cajoling and begging you to want me, but I've had enough. I'm done trying—humiliating myself time and again—for what? A hazy teen fantasy of what might have been, but—"

"Do you ever stop talking?" He swept his free hand under her hair, pulling her close for a kiss that moseyed through her like a warm-honey river. "When I ran into you at the drugstore today, I thought you were the last person I wanted to see. But then I caught a glint of sun in your hair and it terrified me for even a second to think Henry may have been sick, and all my reasons to steer clear of you took a backseat to my selfish reasons for wanting to be with you. You're stubborn and bossy and sexy as hell. And Lord help me but there's nothing I'd rather do than marry you—if you and this little guy will still have me?"

Macy couldn't speak past the knot in her throat, so she nodded, then kissed Wiley, hoping he didn't care that her lips were flavored with tears.

"Let's elope," he said. "Your dad already put it out there that he can't stand me, so—"

"It's not that," she assured. "He respects you a lot, but worries—" She laughed. "Who am I trying to fool? You're right. Let's elope. There's a gorgeous lodge on Mount Karasic that does sunrise weddings. I looked into it for my first. They arrange the licenses and everything. We can ask Wendy to take Henry, Doc Carthage to watch the animals, and make a minivacation out of it. When we get back, we'll make our big announcement at the picnic. Dad will have to be happy for us, right?"

"Not necessarily, but I'm game if you are."

He drew her into a hug. "This is going to be great, right?"

If he had to question that fact, then should they be getting married? Alarm bells pealed in her mind, but Macy clung to him anyway, hoping she was just imagining the boozy smell on his breath.

THE NEXT MORNING, Wiley waited until he was sober enough to drive, then fed his animals and grabbed Blinkie from Macy's. He needed to drive him into town for Doc Carthage to watch Blinkie while he and Macy were gone. Pancake and the cat, horse and goats would be happier at home, but this mutt was high-maintenance.

In anticipation of the Fourth of July, Eagle Ridge's roads

had already swelled with tourist traffic. This time of year, the lake and national forest were a big draw for campers, and even though he'd never been a fan, he had to admit his hometown did a bang-up job of celebrating the holiday.

Flags had been hung from every telephone pole, lamp-post and porch pillar. Flowerboxes and gardens had been planted with geraniums, impatiens and lobelia. For anyone passing through, they must see Eagle Ridge as quintes-sential small-town America, but for him, driving past the liquor store, making plans to stop by after dropping off the dog, the place served as the keeper of his dirty secret.

He shouldn't mix booze with his meds. It was kind of a no-brainer, but what else could he do? To keep up nor-mal appearances with Macy, he now took nearly double his prescribed dosage, yet at times that still wasn't enough to mask the pain. Which begged the question, how was he planning on hiding all of this from his soon-to-be wife? Was it even fair of him to subject her to this big of a per-sonal mess?

Not really. He feared that when it came to his pain meds, he already had a problem, but then he selfishly wondered if hooking up with Macy might be the perfect option for recovery? He hadn't realized how much he'd miss her or what a stabilizing influence she and Henry played in his life until having been forced to go cold turkey without her.

For their new family, Wiley planned to gradually wean himself from the booze and meds. It wouldn't be easy, but he'd do anything for Macy and Henry.

If it hadn't been for Macy convincing Wiley to try the painkillers, he would have never known just how effective they could be. It truly had been a miracle, and he'd been too stubborn to even try. He owed her for that.

*Enough to marry her? Do you even love her? Hell, for that matter, do you even know what real love is?*

His gut fisted. He might not love her, but he sure did like her kissing and cooking. Plus, Henry was a cutie. Lots of folks based marriages on less.

In ten minutes, he'd left the worst of the traffic behind to pull his truck into Doc's veterinary clinic.

"As I live and breathe." Mable, Doc's longtime secretary and assistant, greeted Wiley at the door. The place smelled of antiseptic and fur. The dogs boarded in back provided constant barking background noise. "If it isn't Wiley James all grown up and looking more attractive than the devil's playground on a Saturday night."

"Thank you." He removed his cowboy hat before kissing her cheek. Hard to believe she'd occasionally dated his grandfather. Time sure marched on. "You're not looking too shabby yourself. I'm liking this blond hair."

"Oh, stop." Her cheeks flushed with pleasure. "You're as big a flirt as Buster—God bless his sweet soul."

After hearing about every dog, cat and sheep in the county, she pointed him to the large animal shed where Doc Carthage tended to a horse.

"Never saw this coming," Doc said when Wiley shook his hand and told him the news. "I'm not saying I don't wholeheartedly approve—just that the engagement and wedding came on a bit sudden, don't you think?"

"I suppose…" Wiley rubbed between Blinkie's ears to steady his shaky hands. "But Macy's a good girl. It's high time I make an honest woman of her before some other cowboy snatches her up."

Doc chuckled. "Guess that's one way of putting it. Would I be right in assuming you asked her daddy's permission?"

"Why? She's a grown woman, fully capable of making her own decisions."

"True." Doc fastened the latch on the bay mare's stall,

then made a note in her chart before taking the dog from Wiley. "But her daddy may not see it in the same light. To keep the peace, you might think about pumping the brakes on this shindig. Just sayin'…"

"With all due respect, once Steve Shelton recognizes I only have honorable intentions toward his daughter and grandson, I'll bet he'll come around."

Doc's wary sigh signaled he wasn't so sure.


"You do know this is crazy?" Wendy gave Henry a sugar cookie, then dragged Macy into her hectic shop's back-room.

"Getting married?" Macy set Henry's diaper bag and suitcase filled with other baby essentials next to the play-pen where Wendy had put him.

He'd already found a stuffed owl to chew. The face he made when his tongue touched the fur was priceless. How could Macy leave him for two nights?

"No, hon." Wendy washed her hands at the island's industrial sink. "I'm talking about your upcoming trip to Mars. Of course, I'm talking about your wedding. It's nuts!"

"You wouldn't be saying that if you were about to marry the ultimate man of your dreams. How long have I crushed on the boy?"

Wendy sighed. "That's just it. Wiley's hardly a boy, and a lot happened in the years he's been gone—for both of you. Honestly, I think you're still hurting from Rex, and out to prove any man would want you. And Wiley? Who knows what goes through that head?"

"Knock it off. How can you be so down on Wiley when you barely even know him? I'm sorry if he was short with you, but that's only because back then, he was in constant pain. Now that it's under control, he's charming. When you're around him more, you'll—"

"That's just it—I'd love to give him a second chance, but how can I when you two are slinking off to elope? Can you imagine how devastated your mom and dad will be?"

"I think the more accurate description of their reaction will be relief. They're probably still paying off my first wedding, and I feel terrible about that. But this time around, everything's different. I'm not some moon-eyed girl in love with the idea of being a homemaker, wife and mom."

"Of course, you are—only this time, even worse! You're not marrying Wiley, but his legend. You remember him from his glory days. Tight Wranglers and that cocky smile and his great-big bull-riding belt buckle that he won his sophomore year of high school. But now, he's damaged goods, he—"

"Don't you dare poke fun at his disability."

"This isn't about his leg, Macy, but what happened up here…" She tapped her temple. "The poor guy had to have been through hell. Are you sure he's made peace with it? Lots of vets never do."

"Forget I asked you to watch Henry. He'll be better off with me." Macy turned to get him when Wendy pulled her back.

"I'm sorry. Please don't be mad. Forget I said anything. I'm worried about my friend. Rex put you through hell and the last thing I want is for you to go through something potentially worse."

"Worse than infidelity?" Macy laughed. "Not quite sure what that would be."

Wendy crushed her in a hug. "I pray you never find out, and that this marriage is everything you've ever hoped for."

Returning to the mountain, to Wiley, to begin the first

chapter of her new life, Macy hoped for the same, but her churning stomach made her fear her friend might be right.

Did she need to step back and think about what she was doing for at least one hot minute? Or did she plunge headfirst into what could be her life's greatest blessing?

Sadly, by the time she knew the answers to those questions, it might already be too late to avoid emotional ruin.

# *Chapter Thirteen*

That night, Wiley held Macy in his arms, and felt as if he might be sick. They danced beneath a starry sky, accompanied by a homegrown honky-tonk band playing on Big Sky Ranch's patio stage. The setting returned him to his graduation party, to O'Mally's, where they'd shared their first dance, but that's where the similarities ended. Now, he was all grown up and didn't have a clue how to be a good man—let alone, husband.

He breathed Macy in—the strawberry scent of her hair and that special something his soul recognized as her. That afternoon, they'd gotten their marriage license and rings, and at dawn, before God, a preacher and a panoramic mountain view, they would become husband and wife.

This wedding felt like a train wreck waiting to happen—and that wasn't just his pills and a half-dozen secret shots of Jim Beam talking. Getting hitched would bring the two of them full circle. Growing up, she'd always been his shadow. They'd been each other's first fishing buddies and swimming buddies and he'd be a liar if he didn't admit to being damned curious to what all else they could be good at together in bed. But this union was about more than satisfying a curious itch. Her ex had already hurt her, and if he didn't get his act together to stop taking the drugs, Wiley would only compound her heartache.

The once honorable SEAL in him felt lousy about filling her with false hope for a marriage based on truth and love and a possibly bright shared future.

"Isn't this place amazing?" Her words tumbled in a warm puff against his neck. "We were lucky to get rooms on such short notice." The pine log lodge had been built in 1911 for an East Coast shipping tycoon, high atop Mount Karasic. From this vantage, moonlight bathed virtually the entire Beartooth Range.

"You did good," he agreed.

"I feel kind of guilty."

"About leaving Henry?" He spun her, riding out the pain of his romantic gesture.

"A little. But mostly, not telling Mom and Dad. I'm sure they'd love to be here."

"Want me to call them? Invite them up?" *Please refuse that offer.* His pulse raced for the few seconds it took her to make a decision. This charade was bad enough for him to tackle on his own. Toss her family into the mix, and he'd run for the hills—only, that might be kind of tough, considering his bad leg and the fact that they were already on top of a mountain.

"You're sweet to ask, but no. Dad seems to think you might be damaged from what you went through. Once you're already my husband, he'll be forced to get to know you without bringing along his preconceived theories about your mental well-being."

"That was quite a mouthful." He dipped her back, forcing his facial expression to remain mellow when he wanted to scream. He needed another pill. Or a drink. Preferably, both. "Good to know my future father-in-law thinks I'm a head case."

"Lucky for you—" she stopped dancing to deliver a kiss

"—there are only two members of the Shelton family you have to please. Henry, and me."

The song ended and Wiley struggled for the right words. When he couldn't find any, he settled on kissing Macy, then excusing himself. Before he could work on making her happy, he had to squelch this pain.

"Sure you don't want to come in?" Just inside the honeymoon suite, Macy tried striking a seductive, beckoning pose, but ended up laughing. She hated that Wiley insisted on separate rooms for the night, but applauded his old-fashioned gesture. "Sorry. I meant to look irresistible—not like a clown."

"You look beautiful." He drew her into his arms for a lingering kiss that left no doubt he'd rather stay. "Take tonight to make sure you're solid with this decision."

"Wait—" She searched his face. "Is that your polite way of telling me you're having second thoughts?"

"Not at all." He kissed the tip of her nose. "I just think you need this space. All of this has happened pretty fast—not that I'm complaining. So, with that said, enjoy this great room, and think of me slumming it downstairs." He winked.

She needed to feel her lips against his once more before calling it a night, so she wrapped her arms around his neck, gliding her fingers into his hair, drawing him toward her for a lingering promise of the shared lifetime yet to come.

"Good night," she said.

"Sweet dreams." With one last kiss, he gave her a light push into her room and then shut the door.

For an instant, her every instinct screamed to chase after him, because his leaving didn't feel right and his tongue tasted boozy. But then she forced a deep breath, and looked at the magnificent space and realized what a gift Wiley had given.

She did need this lone night to remind herself she wasn't just a mom or soon-to-be-wife, but *herself.* How long had it been since she'd had time to soak in the tub or stare at the stars?

Tonight, she'd do both.

The room was opulent to the extreme. Whereas her cabin felt cozy, but sometimes claustrophobic with its low ceilings and small spaces, this vaulted space soared. Come morning, the wall of windows would offer a gasp-worthy mountain view. But for now, she enjoyed the small fire housekeeping had made in the stone hearth, and the way the armchair she'd sat in was deep enough to bring on instant relaxation.

How amazing was this whole turn of events?

She hopped up from the chair and raced to the king-size bed. Wrapping herself in the faux-fur throw, she jumped on the cranberry-colored floral spread, giggling like a schoolgirl.

Tired, she collapsed onto the pillowy mattress, but refused to stop smiling. How could she, when her every dream was coming true?

"DO YOU HAVE the ring?"

"I'm sorry, what?" Wiley had temporarily zoned out on his vows. The views were that spectacular—not just the mountains, but his bride. To ensure pain didn't cause him to ruin Macy's special day, he'd taken four pills.

The preacher cleared his throat. "The ring? I'll need you to slip it on Macy's finger."

"Oh, sure. Right." Wiley took it from the front pocket of his best jeans. After they'd gotten their rings at a shopping center jeweler, he'd been ordered to stay in the truck while she'd run into a department store for her dress. Instead of doing as she'd told him, he'd doubled back to buy her a fancy engagement ring. "Here you go, only looks like your wedding ring found a friend."

She gasped. "Wiley! What did you do?"

Her hand trembled while he slipped on her rings. He leaned in to kiss her. "For all the tasty meals you've cooked for me, baby, you deserve the biggest diamond I could find." He punctuated his sentence with a nice, juicy kiss.

The preacher cleared his throat. "Could we please hold off on the smooches until after the ceremony?"

"Oh, sure. Sorry." Wiley stepped back from his bride.

The rest of the ceremony passed in a fog, and then Macy was crying, and they were kissing before the rising sun, and the whole world rose before them.

"I didn't know life could be this good," she said.

"It's only going to get better," he promised.

The lodge had prepared a big breakfast spread. Pancakes, biscuits and gravy, sausage and bacon and eggs, along with fresh fruit cut into fancy shapes that made Macy's smile all the brighter.

The lodge's other guests formed a receiving line and fussed over Macy's dress and hair. Wiley thanked them all from the bottom of his heart for helping to make her day special.

When he finally got his bride alone at their table for two that had been set up beside the steaming pool, he couldn't stop staring. "You look so freakin' pretty."

"Thank you." She raised her champagne to him, then took a sip. "You're not so bad yourself."

"You're the real star." He held out his hand for her, and when their fingers touched, the erotic jolt damn near had him tossing her over his shoulder to take back to their room. "You picked a good dress."

"You picked a good ring." She released him to hold out her hand, letting her diamond catch the sun. "I don't need it, but I sure do like it."

"I'm glad. That was the plan." They ate in companionable silence, taking in each other and the majestic view of snow-capped peaks and fog-shrouded valleys. The air was clean and crisp with the promise of warmth and the scent of the nearby pine forest.

"What are we going to do today?" she asked.

"I talked to the concierge, and he set up a couple of things. First, we're taking a champagne hike, then—"

"Are you sure you feel up for that?"

"Sure. Why wouldn't I?"

"Your leg?"

He waved off her concern. "Let me worry about it. If we only get one day for a honeymoon, I want it to be good. So after the hike, we're renting a boat and having a late lunch on the lake. When's the last time you went sailing?"

"Try never. But I'm game to try."

"Good. After breakfast, we'll change clothes, then get started."

"Okay, but…" She put the strawberry she'd been about to eat on the side of her plate. "Isn't there something you'd rather do?"

"Like what?" He couldn't imagine cramming one more activity into their day.

"You know…" She pressed the issue—literally—by placing her suddenly bare foot on his crotch. "Are you mean enough to make me come out and say it?"

He coughed.

"Is there some reason you don't want to…"

"No. Not at all." Only there was. His stupid pride preferred not to talk about it, but now that they were married, he supposed the issue might be tough to hide.

"Wait—" She glanced around to make sure none of the other guests were within earshot. "You don't have an issue with getting it…*up*?" She reddened when his horndog little cowboy decided to giddyup against the sole of her foot.

"No. No way."

"Good." She smiled. "But even if you did. We could work through it. So what's wrong?"

"All right…" He exhaled. "I wanted to wait until after dark to make this marriage official because my leg isn't the way it used to be when we swam together as kids."

"Let me get this straight—you're stalling because you're afraid I'll be put off by a few scars?" She put down her fork to glare. "It hurts that you think I'm so shallow."

"You don't understand. We're not talking about a few little scars, Mace. My leg was barely saved from amputation. It's an ugly mess. Hell…" He downed his champagne. "Part of me feels guilty for letting you marry me without first sampling the goods."

"Good." She laughed. "Then we're even, because I feel the same. I mean, how many brides do you know who did the proposing?"

He laughed, too, which felt cleansing. Truth be told, spending last night alone hadn't been so much about her, but him working up the courage to see this thing through. He wasn't sure why she wanted to marry him, or what she even saw in him that she found likable. Standing her up at the altar would have been doing her a favor, but as tenderhearted as she was, he also knew it would have gutted her, and he respected her too much to bring her that kind of pain.

*Oh—and you think once she discovers she's married an alcoholic drug addict, she'll be happy?*

From behind them, someone popped a champagne cork.

The sudden noise startled him to the point that he almost grabbed Macy to take cover beneath the table. *Shit.*

Realizing the only pending danger was in his head, he poured fresh bubbly for them both, then proposed a toast. "Here's to the trickster in both of us."

"I'll drink to that, but only if you promise to take me upstairs for a proper bridal ravishing."

He winked. "I think that could be arranged."

IN THEIR SUITE, the daytime view was everything Macy had known it would be, yet she only had eyes for her husband.

Like he had the night before, he ushered her into the room, but this time he followed, closing the door behind him.

He was her every fantasy come to life in new Wranglers, black boots and a starched white button-down. He'd combed his longish hair back for the occasion, and even groomed his stubble. His dark eyes pierced straight through, making her want him a hundred different ways. She had never desired a man more.

She sucked in a swift breath, willing her runaway pulse to slow when she wasn't quite sure how to make the next move. But then Wiley approached, holding out his hands, and brandishing that sexy-slow grin she'd always adored.

"Ready for this?" he asked.

She nodded. "I think so."

"Want music?"

She shook her head.

"More champagne?"

"No…"

"This?" He stepped around behind her, unzipping her chaste white dress. She'd picked it because of the old-fashioned scoop neckline and long, flared skirt. It made her feel as if she'd stepped back in time. She couldn't be much more nervous than if she was a virgin all over again.

His warm knuckles grazed her cool back, and she shivered.

He pressed warm kisses down her spine. "Cold?"

"A little." She held up her bodice. The dress had a built-in bra, so beneath it, she wore nothing but lacy pale blue panties.

"Are these your something blue?" He'd kissed his way to them.

"Yes."

He rose to roll the dress from her shoulders. "What's your something old?"

"Grandma's pearls."

"New is your dress." It landed in a puddle on the floor.

She nodded.

"Which leaves your something borrowed." He took off his shirt.

The breadth of his chest left her tongue-tied.

Feeling shy, she held her hands over her breasts.

"Mace? Borrowed?"

"Oh—my hair comb. It's Wendy's."

"Pretty." He gave it a tug, spilling her long hair about her shoulders. "Just like you." He kissed a new trail across her collarbone and then up her throat, in the process pulling down her hands, easing his fingers between hers.

Sun slanted through the wall of windows in a wide swath, and he lifted her only to set her in the spot where it met the foot of the bed. The sunshine's warmth calmed her nerves and reminded her she had nothing to fear.

This was Wiley.

Her oldest, dearest friend. And now, her husband.

"The years have been a lot kinder to you than me." As if surveying a buffet, he stepped back to appraise her.

Shyness kicked in, and she once again raised her hands, but he drew them down.

"Let me see." He ran his hand across her rounded belly and along the in-and-out curve of her hips.

"You know how you feel bashful about your leg? I have the same hang-ups. Having a baby didn't do me any favors. I still could lose thirty pounds and my stretch marks are—"

He kissed her quiet. "Stop putting down my wife."

"Your *wife*." She let that sink in. How many times had she written *Mrs. Wiley James* and *Mrs. Macy James* across the insides of her notebook when she'd been bored in algebra class?

"That's right. Which means I'm now legally allowed to do this..." He trailed his tongue along the underside of one breast, then the other before suckling so hard on her nipple that moisture pooled between her legs.

"Yes, please," she practically purred, happy for him to do whatever he wanted all day long.

She quickly forgot to be shy when he made her feel if she didn't soon have him inside her, she'd lose what little was left of her sanity.

He removed his jeans and boxers, then joined her on the bed. A glimpse of his poor leg was all she needed to understand why he hadn't wanted her to see. The scarring was bad enough for her to realize the fresh injury must have been unfathomable. The ghost of what he'd been through tightened her throat, but for his sake, she wouldn't let sorrow take away one speck of this moment's joy.

He pressed his lips to hers as he cupped her belly, then he said, "Hold up. Let me grab a condom."

"No. I'm good."

"Sure?"

She nodded.

She'd barely wondered if he wasn't sure—about conceiving a child with her—when he eased down the length of her, lavishing attention to her belly, and then lower. By the time he drew her panties down, tossing them to join her dress on the floor, she was more than ready to have him on top of her, and he obliged.

Her worries about how they'd connect without hurting his leg were unfounded. The deeper he drove, the more connected with him she felt. She dug her fingers into his back, urging him on with each thrust.

It had been so long since she'd been with a man that she felt brand-new. Wiley made lovemaking fresh and clean and pure.

When her orgasm struck, the intensity brought tears.

Wiley stiffened and moaned. He kissed her cheeks and forehead and finally, her lips. "You taste like tears. Everything okay?"

She nodded. "I'm happy. So happy."

"I'm glad." He cupped her cheek, and she leaned into his touch, wishing she could encapsulate this wondrous feeling and keep it always with her.

He kissed the crown of her head. "Ready for our hike?"

"Not quite yet..."

Leisurely kisses led to making love all over again, and then soaking in the roomy tub. By the time they'd both dressed for the rest of the day, it was practically time for lunch.

"When were we supposed to meet our guide?" Macy asked on the way down the lodge's wide staircase.

"Two hours ago."

She cast him an over-the-shoulder grin. "Oops."

He landed a light smack to her behind. The newly emerged naughty girl in her liked it! What other surprises would her marriage bring?

## Chapter Fourteen

The waterfall was pretty and majestic and all that, but the powerful roar made Wiley uneasy. The inescapable noise brought back the past he'd worked hard to forget.

While waiting for their guide, Macy had called Wendy to check on Henry. Wiley used the moment alone to take two more pain pills. As amazing as their morning together had been, it was also that exhausting. Thank God, his bride hadn't noticed him break out in a cold sweat from exertion.

He was pathetic.

Did she love him? Or feel sorry for him?

He honestly couldn't tell.

But relief was kicking in. And that was good.

He closed his eyes, soaking in the sun, willing away images fighting to overtake the happy day.

*The ground beneath him trembled. Fire was every-where. Smoke made it impossible to breathe. He clawed at his throat, but there was no air. Crow? Where is he? I have to find—*

"Wiley, scoot closer. I want a great picture to frame and put on the mantel."

His exit from the grisly scene was slow. *There was so much blood. Why wouldn't the ground stop shaking?*

"Wiley? Come closer. What's wrong? You look like you're in another world."

"No. I'm good." Crow and those poor kids were long in their graves and in a better place where chaos didn't rule.

He glanced up to find their guide waving him next to Macy, so he slipped his arm around her for what he hoped was the quintessential honeymoon pose. For her sake, he had to keep it together. Soon enough, they'd leave the waterfall's roar to enjoy the rest of the day on a nice, peaceful boat, where he could hopefully grab a nap.

"Where do you two want me to set up your champagne and strawberries?" the guide asked. The tall kid looked to be in his early twenties. He had short blond hair and too many teeth.

"I'm not hungry," Wiley said. "Let's save it for the lake."

"Aw, but it's so pretty here." Macy had her hands on her hips. "What's your hurry?"

"It's too loud," he complained. Without sounding like a freak, how did he adequately convey just how uncomfortable the water's continuous roar made him? "Tomorrow, we'll be with a crowd, but today, I want to be with you."

She wrinkled her nose. "That doesn't make sense. There's not another soul for miles. As soon as Jory heads back to the Jeep, we'll be totally alone."

"Mace…" *I need to go. Now.*

"Okay." She might have agreed, but didn't look happy about it. "But let me take a few more pics."

MACY DIDN'T UNDERSTAND Wiley's rush to escape the scenic view it had taken an hour's hike to find, but since she was now nice and comfy in the cockpit of the luxurious sailboat he'd rented for the rest of the day, she wasn't complaining.

Between the sun's heat and the water lapping against the hull, she'd have taken a relaxing snooze. But who could sleep when it was much more fun to watch Wiley? He'd changed from cowboy boots to deck shoes, but his Wranglers and white T-shirt with a Navy insignia stayed the same, as had his old straw cowboy hat.

"Is that the same hat you wore during your brief, but glorious bull-riding career?"

"So what if it is?" He tugged it lower on his forehead.

"I can't believe you've kept it all this time. I'm surprised it hasn't rotted."

"In a few paces it has." He poked his finger through a hole in the side of the brim.

"Want a new one for a wedding gift?"

"Nope. I like this one just fine. Reckon I've had it just about as long as you."

"You're awful!" She lunged across the cockpit for him, but he escaped to wield that sexy grin from in front of the cabin door. "Although, I guess since it was only this morning that I technically had you, maybe the hat's been with me longest?"

"Is it too late for an annulment?"

"Yes." He was beside her, pushing her braids over her shoulders to nuzzle her neck.

At first, she laughed because his whiskers tickled, but then he turned his attentions to lower parts of her body and she no longer felt like laughing. After a brief pause in the action for Wiley to lower the sail, they launched further explorations below deck.

TWO DELICIOUS HOURS PASSED, and aside from the birth of her son, Macy couldn't remember ever having been happier. If it wasn't for her excitement to have Henry back in her arms, she could have stayed on this boat forever.

Alas, they were due back at the rental dock by six, so while she tidied the cabin, Wiley got them back underway.

When she hopped from the cabin back to the cockpit, she noticed him in the bow, favoring his leg. Was he hurting? Guilt gripped her stomach. Had she been a more thoughtful wife, she would have skipped the hike. No wonder he'd wanted to leave the falls. He'd probably been in pain. His medicine seemed to work so well that she forgot he'd even been injured.

The lake twisted for thirty miles through mountain passes, and her husband looked equally at home at the helm of this boat as he did on land. "Did you learn to sail in the Navy?"

He laughed. "Not so much. The boats we used were a little more high-tech. My friend Raleigh came from a *la-di-da* Charleston family and used to sail every weekend we weren't deployed. He liked racing, and sometimes used me for crew." After leaning in for a quick kiss, he winked. "Yacht clubs are great places to pick up chicks. They fall for the cowboy hat every time."

"Ha ha. Too bad for you, you're taken."

He took her hand for a gentle squeeze. "Did we really get hitched this morning?"

"Yes, we did. I'm still pinching myself."

"How mad are your mom and dad going to be?"

"On a scale of one to ten, I'd say we're sitting between a thirty or forty." She wrinkled her nose. "But that's assuming we arrive fashionably late, and Dad's temper has been mellowed by my mom's potato salad, brownies and plenty of beer."

"Sure you want to do this?" The next afternoon, Wiley squeezed Macy's hand. They stood on the street outside her parents' house. Even from half a block down, it was clear the backyard party was already in full swing. Country music played and muted conversations were punctuated with laughter. He'd already taken a couple pain pills while Macy chatted with Wendy, and looked forward to chasing them with a couple beers. "Our honeymoon suite might be booked, but I'm sure we could find someplace else to stay."

"Let's be real. It's the Fourth of July. There's not a lodge, campground or tent available in all of Montana." She swung Henry from his safety seat and into her arms.

"Still. Wouldn't you rather grab a couple steaks and have a quiet celebration at home?"

"Yes." She kissed the baby, then him. "But this has to be done, and it's far better we do it in a group setting than when my folks are alone."

He winced. "That doesn't make me feel better."

"Come on, Mr. James. You'll be fine."

Wiley wished he could be so sure.

Wendy had been putting on makeup in her car, but she'd now caught up with Macy. Wiley hung back while the ladies chatted their way into the house.

Before his injury, he'd felt most at home in a crowd. The more the merrier. But now, he preferred being alone—Macy didn't count. Well, of course, she did, but in a different way. She allowed him to be himself.

Inside, he was surprised to find the house hadn't changed much since he'd last been there with his grandfather for a Sunday supper. There was a new recliner in the living room's far corner, and the brown shag carpet had been swapped for short beige. The place smelled of home cooking with a hint of fresh paint.

He spied a keg on the kitchen counter, along with a stack of red Solo cups, and helped himself, downing the whole thing before Macy and her friend finished inspecting Henry's new duds of denim overalls and a red plaid shirt. He even had new mini-cowboy boots. The little guy sure was a cutie.

Since the girls were still talking, he had another beer—strictly to settle his nerves.

"Wiley! You came!" Macy's mom abandoned her empty platter on the kitchen island to wrap him in a hug. "I swear you got even more handsome since the last time I saw you."

"Thank you, ma'am." He removed his straw hat. "You're mighty easy on the eyes, yourself."

"Still a flirt, I see." She blushed. "Where in the world is that daughter of mine with my grandson?"

"Oh—she and Wendy are in the living room. Macy and I—we, well, we rode together."

"Really? Are you two an item?"

He cleared his throat. "Ah, you might say that."

"Mom, hi." Macy rounded the corner.

Adrianne Shelton only had eyes for her grandson. "There's my sweet ray of sunshine. Come here and give your *glamma* a big hug."

Henry nearly jumped from Macy's arms to reach his grandma and make a beeline for her shiny rhinestone flag earrings.

*"Glamma?"* Wiley asked Macy under his breath.

She shrugged. "It's her thing. She heard it on a reality show and it stuck."

Nodding, he asked, "How do you want to play this?"

"Cool. Very cool. Let me do the talking. We'll first break it to Mom, then—"

"Macy Jane Shelton, what is that on your—" Macy's mom gasped, covering her mouth with her free hand. "Did you two?" Tears shone in her eyes.

Macy nodded. "Please, don't be mad. We wanted to tell you, but with Daddy being—"

"Mad? I'm not angry, just confused. Last I heard, you two weren't speaking. Isn't this a bit sudden?" She pulled both of them into an awkward group hug. "How did this even happen? And why weren't we invited to the wedding?"

"Who's married?" Steve entered through the patio's sliding glass door, but stopped when he saw new guests had arrived. "Wendy and—Wiley. I didn't know you were coming."

"Nice to see you again, sir." Wiley took off his hat again to shake Steve's hand. Thank the good Lord above that the meds were finally kicking in. "And it's the darnedest thing, but…" He slipped his arm around Macy's waist. His pulse hadn't beat this fast since the last time he'd faced enemy fire. "Your daughter and I got hitched yesterday morning up at a nice lodge near Lake Levasseur."

"No." Steve dumped the keg he'd been carrying on the counter. From the thud, Wiley guessed it was empty. He selfishly hoped Macy's dad had drunk more than his fill. "Do not tell me you just married my daughter without so much as running it by her mother and me? Please, tell me that's not the case, or by God, I'll—"

"Daddy, stop!" Macy left Wiley's side to go to her father. "I'm happy. Yes—this was sudden, but right. Why can't you be happy?"

"I can't be happy, because my beautiful daughter is clearly in way over her head. Wiley, I mean no disrespect, son, but as a fellow serviceman, I understand you've faced nothing but an uphill battle since you've been home. I'm sorry about your injuries. Really, I am, but the boys down at the VFW say you're—"

"Look." Wiley searched for just the right words to diffuse this awkward situation. "When I first got back to town, I'll be the first to admit I was a bastard. Ladies, pardon my language, but plain and simple, I was a mean son of a bitch, and didn't give a damn who knew it. When your VFW friends kept stopping by the cabin to ask me to join their group, I told them point-blank to get the hell off my land, and never come back. But that wasn't me, sir. Your daughter—your beautiful, kind, sweet daughter and grandson changed me…" His voice cracked, and the gratitude he felt for Macy and her son overwhelmed him to the point that he feared he might not be able to speak. But he had to. He had to make Macy's folks, Wendy, hell—the whole damn town—see that Macy had made everything better by convincing him to start taking the meds his doctor had prescribed. "Macy and Henry, they're too good for me, but I'm gonna try to do better. Macy and I are thinking of starting a trail riding operation, and once I take over caring for all the animals, she should have more time for the baby and those sweaters she makes."

"Man to man?" Steve's eyes also welled with tears. He swiped at them, then cleared his throat. "I can't deny this news makes me sad…" He patted his chest. "Try seeing this from my point of view. I don't know the extent of your injuries, but from what I hear, your leg was messed up pretty bad. Are you on permanent disability? Would you be able to raise my grandson in the capacity of a real father?"

The question struck Wiley as an insult. "Forgive me, sir, if this comes out wrong, but I have friends who came back from Afghanistan with no legs, and they do just fine by their sons and daughters. So yeah, considering all I have is an occasionally cranky knee, don't you worry. Macy and Henry will be A-okay under my watch."

"What about love?" Macy's mother asked. "I haven't heard that kind-of-important word leave either of your mouths."

*"Mom…"* Macy scowled. "Please, can't you and Dad stop with all the questions and be happy for me? For *us*?"

Adrianne blew her nose on a red, white and blue napkin. Her husband extended his hand for Wiley to shake. "I'm far from thrilled about the way this marriage came about, but what's done is done, so for my grandson's sake, let's all try making the best of it."

"Agreed." Wiley didn't realize how badly he'd missed his father until connecting with Macy's dad. He wasn't sure why he'd even agreed to this whole marriage idea—maybe just because he got a kick out of making Macy smile. But now that he was in, he really would try harder—at everything. He'd get off the drugs and get their trail-riding business up and running.

In short, he'd do everything in his power to make his dad proud. Or wait—Steve was Macy's dad. His meds had gotten all mixed up with the beer, and damned if for an instant, he hadn't felt as if he was back in his own father's hold.

Tears and hugs abounded, and then Steve led the procession outdoors where he clanged a wooden spoon against the side of a full keg. When that didn't get everyone's attention, he whistled. "Hey! All of y'all pipe down! I have an announcement!"

The crowd of about fifty stopped their conversations to stare. Wiley felt their eyes on him, questioning his very sanity, but Steve put his arm around his shoulder, as if claiming him as his son. Raising his chin, Wiley pressed his lips tight to keep from shedding more tears.

Steve pulled his daughter in on his opposite side, then said to the crowd, "If you don't have a cup, you'd best get one, because I have a toast."

A murmur swept through the crowd.

Adrianne handed her husband a fresh beer, then poured one for herself.

Wendy gave one to Wiley and Macy.

"To my daughter and her brand-spanking-new husband, Wiley James. Now, a lot of you probably remember I had a beef with the boy a ways back when he tried kissing my little girl."

All present chuckled.

"But as long as he keeps making my Macy happy, then I'll agree to let bygones be bygones. That said—" he looked directly into Wiley's eyes "—if I get so much as a hint of my precious girl being unhappy, you're gonna have hell to pay. We clear?"

"Yessir."

"All right, then. Welcome to the family." He raised his glass. "To Mr. and Mrs. Wiley James!"

From there, the afternoon passed in a blur.

Wiley felt reborn.

Surrounded by the folks who had known his parents and grandparents, carrying Henry as the boy tugged his hair, the world once again became Wiley's playground, and he owed it all to Macy for pushing him to take his meds. Granted, at the moment he probably had taken a few too many, but she was a good woman for getting him back in the game.

His eyes sought her out amongst the crowd, and found her dancing to a silly country song with Doc Carthage, who'd brought Blinkie. The dog looked as if he was smiling to be back in Macy's arms, and really, who could blame him?

Wiley excused himself from a few of his old school friends and their parents to be with his bride. "Doc, it's good to see you. I would thank you for watching my brood, but since they're all yours anyway…" He raised his eyebrows and smiled.

"Oh, no," Doc said with a good-natured chuckle. "That motley crew is all yours. And if the goats and Lulu and Charlie and his angels got into your garden while you were gone, I had nothing to do with it." After a quick wink, he poked grinning Henry's belly before heading back to the buffet.

"Speaking of gardens—" Macy wiped a chocolate frosting smudge from her son's chubby cheek. "We haven't discussed living arrangements. With Henry's nursery set up at my place, I kind of assumed we'd land there, but if you'd rather—"

"Your place is fine." Wiley pulled her to him when a slow song played. He was so high on life, swaying with his bride, that he could almost ignore the pain creeping up his leg like a dark vine. It squeezed him, and his raw nerves occasionally twitched as if pricked by thorns.

At the end of the dance he excused himself to head to the john, but what he really needed to do was take more medicine. He now needed upwards of ten to twelve pills a day to maintain status quo, when his prescribed dosage was six. His supply was perilously low, so first thing in the morning, he'd need to make a pharmacy run.

Upon returning to the party, he found Macy waiting for him, but Henry was gone. The booze mixed with his medicine had made him foggy on the day's finer details, and he couldn't remember if he might have accidentally left the baby somewhere.

"Where's Henry?" he asked. "Is he okay?"

"He's fine." She eyed him funny before unscrewing the cap on the bottle of Coke she carried, then took a long drink. "Right up there with my mom and dad." She pointed to where her parents and seemingly everyone else crossed the backyard to get to the street.

Steve steered a wheelbarrow loaded with blankets and giggling Henry.

"Where's everyone going?" Wiley asked. "Is that safe?"

"Of course, it's safe." She took his hand, leading him in the same direction. "Don't you remember there's a short-cut to the high school football stadium at the end of our street? We're all headed to see the fireworks."

He wrinkled his nose. "I don't think that's such a good idea."

"Why not?"

Wiley took a deep breath, needing those pills to kick in—*fast*.

"Wiley?" She paused beneath a streetlight. The yellow glare accentuated shadows under her eyes, making her gaunt. The observation caused him worry. Wiley promised her dad that he would take care of her and her son, and he was a man of his word. *Work, pills. Work.* "Is your leg hurting? If so, Mom's got her phone. I can text her that we're going to hang back at the house."

"No, no. I'm good."

He felt her searching his face, no doubt looking for signs of weakness. But he wasn't weak. He was a warrior. If he'd made it through actual battle, how bad could a few fireworks be?

"Promise?" She was leading him into the darkness beyond the light, and he wasn't just talking about leaving the streetlight's glow. The farther they got from her parents' house, the more his stomach fisted.

## Chapter Fifteen

Macy arched her head back, leaning on Wiley's strong, solid chest to watch the show. For as long as she could remember, Fourth of July nights had been spent in this very spot—on the fifty yard line of Eagle Ridge High's football field, lounging on an old quilt, staring up at the brilliantly lit sky.

The cool evening air smelled of dew and fresh-mown grass and the fireworks' faint sulfur smoke.

Most years, she'd sat with her parents or friends, pining for Wiley. Either she watched him make out with another girl, or, when he was on active duty, she'd prayed for his safety. Her few years with Rex, she'd played at being happy, but until being with Wiley, she now knew she hadn't even been sure what real happiness was.

Here, now—yesterday at the waterfall and on the boat, and most especially, while saying her vows and making love with the man she'd always adored, Macy felt wonderfully, wholly complete.

She sat up to kiss him, to tell him just how happy he made her, when she noticed him flinch from an extra loud shell.

"Sweetie, what's wrong?" Every flash, pop and crackle showed a new expression of terror.

While everyone around them *oohed* and *aahed*, he'd

closed his eyes and tensed, fisting his hands so tightly she couldn't uncurl his fingers to hold his hand.

"Wiley, talk to me. What's going on?"

When he didn't answer, panic set in. Should she call her mom or dad over to help?

"Is your leg hurting?"

He opened his eyes, but seemed to stare right through her.

Terror lodged in her throat when he suddenly jolted, gripping her upper arms to roll himself on top of her. *"Incoming! Take cover!"*

"Wiley, stop! You're hurting me." She squirmed out from under him. "Wake up! Are you having some kind of flashback? Is this PTSD? Let me help. I'll get my dad, and maybe he—"

"Mace? Are you okay? Where's Henry? *We have to get him.*"

"I'm fine, but you're not." She struggled out from under Wiley's weight to sit up. She cupped his dear face with both hands, forcing him to look nowhere but into her eyes. "Wiley, I need you to look at me. *Only at me.* You're *safe.* All of us are *safe.* Henry's with my parents just across the field. I need you to come back to me. *Please.* Can you do that?"

He nodded, but still carried that blank stare, as if his body had been taken over by someone new.

"You are precious to me, do you know that?" Her voice had taken on a near desperate tone. She tried staying calm, but with the explosions more intense than ever, it grew harder to break through his internal wall. Were the fireworks returning him to the time he was wounded? "Wiley, hon, do you have your medicine?"

When he didn't respond, she fished in the pocket of his jeans and found his vial of pills. His supply was low, but she was sure his doctor had given him plenty of refills. She shook two into her palm, then fumbled her hand along the blanket for the bottle of Coke she'd brought along for the show.

She eased the pills past his lips, then held the drink to his mouth. "Do you think you can swallow?"

He nodded and did as she'd told him.

"Good. Thank you. Now, I'm going to need you to stand up, and then walk with me back to the truck. We're going to leave Henry to stay the night with my folks, then you and I are going to spend a nice, quiet night on our mountain, okay?"

He didn't nod or speak, but did stand and take her hand, squeezing her fingers to the point of pain. But she didn't care. She was strong, and for him, she could take it. She just needed to help him through this temporary hurdle and all would be right again.

But if helping Wiley would truly be that easy, why did her heart ache with fear for the man with whom she'd just vowed to spend the rest of her life?

THE NEXT MORNING, Wiley was slow to wake. Even then, he didn't know where he was. His leg hurt like a son of a bitch and he needed a drink and his pills—not necessarily in that order.

He rolled over to find Macy, and it all came rushing back. Telling her folks they'd gotten married. The high of their backyard barbecue and the paralyzing low of the town fireworks show.

Covering his face with his hands, Wiley wished for…

What? What magic bullet would make this nightmare go away? Would a never-ending supply of pain pills or booze help?

Hell, no. He was already on that road to nowhere.

What options did that leave? Even worse? He was almost out of the pills that were the only thing keeping him on the tightrope he was continuously trying to walk.

Marrying Macy had been a huge mistake.

As soon as possible, he needed to tell her she was in over her head, and that their marriage would never work.

"You're awake."

Wiley was startled from his thoughts by Macy reaching across the bed to stroke his hair. Lord help him, he'd forgotten she was even there. "Hey, babe."

"How are you feeling?"

"Good." *Liar.* Because no matter how screwed up he was, he did genuinely care for her, he captured her hand.

"You scared me last night."

*I scared myself.*

"I had Mom and Dad watch Henry, so we could talk."

"There's nothing to talk about. I mean, there's plenty, but not about last night."

He left the bed to somehow make it to the bathroom. His leg pain was indescribable.

He used the facilities, then asked, "Know where I might find my jeans?"

She must have stripped him before going to bed, because he now wore just his boxers. In the glaring sunlight streaming through the windows, his injured leg looked like an ugly red caricature of his former normal limb. He needed to cover it—now. And then he needed his damned pills that he'd last seen in his front pocket.

She'd left the bed, too, and took his jeans from the back of an armchair, then handed them to him. "If you're looking for your medicine, it's on the kitchen counter. Want me to get it for you?"

"No. I can handle it." As badly as he craved masking his ugly scars, he needed pain relief that much more.

She darted around him, meeting him before he'd even made it halfway with a glass of water and two pills.

He'd have rather had three.

His hands shook so badly from the effort of holding himself upright that he slopped water all over his chest. Lord… He looked like a damned fool, and could only imagine what Macy must think.

She took the glass, returned it to the kitchen, then doubled back behind him for his jeans. "Lean on me for support, and I'll help you put these on."

"I can do it." He didn't mean to snap.

"I know you can, but since I'm now your wife, I'm going to help. Deal with it."

"You never should have hitched your wagon to me. I'm a lost cause."

"Oh, stop. You had a rough night, and slept past time for your next round of pain meds. We won't let that happen again. As for your reaction to the fireworks, I did some reading last night after putting you to bed, and I'm guessing you've got PSTD. Post Traumatic Stress Syndr—"

"I know what it is, and I'm fine, Doctor Macy."

"If you could have seen yourself during the show, you'd know you're not fine."

"It was one night." He'd hobbled back to the bed and collapsed. "Give me a sec for my meds to kick in, and I'll be right as rain." He closed his eyes, struggling for the sense of normalcy she deserved. "I was talking to one of Gramps's friends yesterday, and he said he's already seen a few ripe huckleberries. How about we run into town to grab Henry, refill my meds, then we head back here for berry picking?"

"Really?" She stood at the foot of the bed with her hands on her hips.

"What part of that didn't sound good?"

"You're honestly going to sweep what happened last night under the rug? Wiley, you weren't yourself. I don't know who you were. At one point, you told me to take cover. Does that sound normal to you?"

"Drop it, okay? I'm sorry the big fireworks show didn't turn out as idyllic as you'd have liked. From day one, I told you I'm a mess, but you didn't believe me. If you want to get this disaster annulled, I understand."

"Way to stay strong on the for-better-or-worse part of our vows."

"Macy, wake up." He punched his pillow before shoving it behind his head. "How many times do I have to tell you I'm no good for you? The whole thing with the fireworks caught me off guard. The waterfall did, too. The champagne cork at our wedding breakfast. I thought all I had to deal with was my leg pain, but there's more."

"Okay." Arms crossed, she paced the short length of the room. "Then we'll handle all of it together. I think you should make an appointment with a doctor and a therapist, and if you want, I'll go, too. But first, I need coffee. Want a cup?"

"Sure. But I'll get it myself."

"No, you won't."

For once, because he physically had no other option, he followed her request. Eyes closed, he breathed in and out, in and out, willing the medicine to do its job.

Little by little, relief flowed through him. It was warm and seductive, flooding him with well-being until he felt good enough to not only get out of bed, but wander into the kitchen to find Macy.

The coffee smelled wonderful, but not nearly as good as the strawberry-scent of her hair.

Slipping his arms around his wife's waist, he nuzzled what little he could see of her neck in her oddly sexy, long flannel nightgown. "I like you all fuzzy. What've you got on under this massive thing?"

"Great big granny panties you wouldn't be the least bit interested in. Now, back to the matter at hand, I looked up a few names in the phone book—"

"Let me see." He inched up the sides of her gown.

"What? Wiley, no!" She swatted him away. "Please, take this seriously. I think you have a serious problem."

"My only problem right now is getting you out of this nightie …"

"WHERE IS HE NOW?" Wendy asked.

"At the pharmacy. I told him I needed to come here to get one of Henry's shoes. But really, I wanted to run all of this past you. What do you think? Does this sound serious?"

"Probably? Maybe? I don't know. At the party, he was one hundred percent old Wiley. Charming and funny and don't you ever tell him I said this, but sexy as hell. If I was lucky enough to be married to him, I'd also abandon sobering conversation for a morning quickie."

*"Wendy!"* Macy's cheeks superheated as she surveyed the coffeehouse crowd, praying no one had heard her friend's bawdy comment. "You can't say things like that."

"Why not? Wiley made an honest woman out of you, so you're allowed to engage in all kinds of deliciously naughty activities—as much as you want."

"You're just as bad as him."

"Look—" She straightened the individually wrapped shortbread cookies she kept on a silver tray next to the register. "No one was more against this marriage than I. I thought it all happened way too soon. But then I saw the three of you together—the way you were always smiling, and I changed my mind. I think you and Wiley both need each other, and fate brought you together. Sure, Wiley no doubt has issues to work through from his time overseas, but who doesn't? From what I can tell, the guy adores you and your son. Why not give him a pass on whatever happened last night, and enjoy the rest of your life?"

"You're probably right." Macy sighed, then reached for a cookie. "How much are these?"

"For you, free." Macy's friend rounded the corner to give her a much-needed hug. "So have five or six, and then relax. Be happy. You're a newlywed. Everything's going to be fine."

Macy wished she could be so sure.

"WHAT DO YOU MEAN you can't refill it?" The pharmacist was some punk kid straight out of school, and clearly didn't know his ass from a hole in the ground. "I just refilled it last week."

"Right. And now it says on the bottle you have no available refills. But if you don't mind waiting, we can call your doctor, and—"

"I don't have time to wait." Wiley glanced over his shoulder to make sure Macy hadn't entered the suddenly too-tight space.

"Sir, I can make the call right now. As long as your doctor okays your refill, you'll be good to go."

Since there was no one else at the counter, Wiley leaned in. "I got those meds after I was released from a VA hospital back in Virginia. I was supposed to follow up with a doc closer to home, but never did—my bad. But now, I'm in a bind. So could you maybe help me out, and I'll see someone else soon?"

The kid handed Wiley the near-empty bottle. "I'm sorry, sir. My dad's a vet, so I understand that it's sometimes tough getting back into the swing of things, but I'll get you a list of area physicians, and hopefully, one of them can give you an appointment soon."

*Soon?* He had only eight pills, which would barely get him through the day. "Tell you what, go ahead and see about getting ahold of the guy who gave me this prescription."

"Sure." He took back the bottle, then pointed Wiley toward a small waiting area with three metal folding chairs and posters about taking meds as prescribed and washing your hands after sneezing. "Have a seat, and I'll let you know what I find out."

"Great. Thanks." Upon sitting, Wiley wiped his sweaty palms on the thighs of his jeans. Nervous energy escaped him via his fidgety feet. He was supposed to have met back up with Macy by now so they could grab Henry from her folks. This shouldn't be taking so long.

He stood to pace, glancing every so often at the punkass pharmacist who was still on the phone.

Wandering down the infant-care aisle, he grabbed a few toys for Henry, along with four jars of gourmet baby food. His new kid deserved the best—unlike the punk pharmacist.

At the front of the store, he grabbed a basket to use for lugging his purchases.

Macy needed presents, too. Nail polish looked good—Rev-it-Up Red. He found candy bars for her in the next aisle, along with a couple magazines, and a recipe book for one-pot cooking. She liked to cook.

Back at the rear of the store, he found the pharmacist finally off the phone.

"Oh, hey, Mr. James. Great news. I got you one more full week of medication. I'll just need your ID. Your insurance is already on file."

"Great." Wiley set his basket on the counter. Relief

shimmered through him. "I'll need this stuff, too." *But only a week?* At his prescribed dosage, that meant six pills per day, multiplied by seven. Forty-two chances to get things right—no, twenty-one, considering he took two at a time. He now took ten to twelve pills per day, which meant he had three days max to find a doctor—*any* doctor. There was no way he'd find a VA clinic by then—if there was even one within a hundred miles. "I'd appreciate that list of local doctors, too."

"There's only one here in town, but the list has all of them in the area."

"Thanks." Minutes later, Wiley had stashed his purchases in the truck bed—save for his meds. Those, he put in his pocket. He kept the doctor list, too, and used his cell to make an appointment with Dr. Jessie Burke over in Newflower, which was a good twenty miles from prying eyes. As an added benefit, the receptionist said the doctor had had a cancellation, and could see him the next morning at ten.

Spirits bolstered, he bought a Dr. Pepper from a machine outside the pharmacy, then took two pills. For his visit with Macy's parents, he needed to be on top of his game. She said she hadn't told them anything about his meltdown, which he appreciated, but it took a lot for him to maintain the level of normalcy that she, and now her parents, had come to expect.

He wanted to make them proud.

*What about yourself? Are you proud of being an addict?*

He ignored his conscience to admire the gorgeous weather.

The day was fine, with the temperature promising to hit the high seventies, so he walked to Wendy's coffeehouse to find Macy.

The fact that she hadn't left his sorry ass surprised him.

Maybe the even bigger surprise was that he was glad to still have her and Henry with him. When his pain was under control, he got a kick out of being a family man. If he could no longer be a SEAL, maybe being a father and husband was the next best thing? His granddad once told him that raising his father was the most satisfying job he'd ever had. Wiley needed that sense of purpose and belonging.

He needed to feel needed.

Downtown still bustled with tourists. The candy shop had the door open, and the sweet scent of fresh caramel corn made him smile. He used to get stuck taking Macy there after school on Fridays. While waiting for their grandfathers, they'd get ice cream or taffy still warm from the pulling machine.

Did she remember?

He needed her to remember.

At the coffeehouse, he opened the door for the couple leaving, then headed inside.

"Wiley, hi." The way Macy smiled at him made his every problem fade. She was so pretty. From the galaxy of freckles spanning her button nose and cheeks to the sky-blue eyes he could stare into for hours. She'd piled her red corkscrew hair into a messy bun, and as far as he was concerned, he'd never seen her look more beautiful.

"Hey, babe." With his meds working at full capacity, he gravitated into her arms. "Find Henry's shoe?"

"His what? Oh—no. I must have left it somewhere else."

"Hey, Wendy." Wiley waved to Macy's friend.

"Hey, yourself. Get everything you needed at the pharmacy?"

"Sure did. Plus, a whole lot more. That place stocks the damnedest things."

"Hmm..." Wendy worked on a fancy coffee Wiley assumed the burly guy standing at the counter must have ordered. "Guess I've never noticed."

"If you get a chance, you *really* should." High on life and feeling no pain, he winked. "*Great* stuff."

Macy and her friend shared a look. If he hadn't been feeling so Zen, he might have wondered what it was about.

## *Chapter Sixteen*

"There are the two lovebirds," Adrianne teased the second Macy and Wiley walked through the door, giving them both big hugs.

Macy shut the front door. "I told you last night wasn't like *that*. We both needed to catch up on our sleep."

"Uh-huh…" She winked before returning to her seat at the dining room table, where she was already scrapbooking her Fourth of July photos. "Protest all you want, but I didn't just ride into town on the back of a turnip truck. I used to be young."

"Look at you, little man." Wiley gravitated toward Henry who'd pulled himself up on the playpen's edge. "You've got some impressive skills. High-five." Macy needed to hold tight to her frustration with Wiley. She needed to watch for further signs that something else might be wrong with his physical or mental state. But how could she when at this moment, watching him interact with her son, felt so incredibly right?

He'd bought all those silly gifts from the drugstore, and then the two of them reminisced about how much trouble he'd gotten in for sticking his hand in the candy store's taffy-pulling machine all because Macy dared him.

In the future, if he showed the slightest indication something was wrong, she'd address the heck of out it then. But for now, like Wendy suggested, Macy chose to put all worries aside to be happy.

"Hey." Steve entered through the kitchen's sliding glass door. "I didn't know we had company."

"Hi, Dad." Macy gave him a hug. "What have you been doing? You're all sweaty."

"Don't ask," Adrianne called from the dining room. "I told him it was too soon, but he insisted."

"Now I'm really curious," Macy said.

"This was supposed to be a surprise—" Steve left her to get a bottled water from the fridge "—but a few weeks back, for Henry, I ordered a DIY backyard castle fort kit from an online place. It's gonna be awesome—it has swings and a slide and a sandbox moat."

"Dad, Henry can't even walk."

"Maybe not now, but he's getting there. Look at him." Clasping the playpen's edge, her son danced and giggled. Could life possibly get much sweeter?

"Sounds awesome," Wiley said. "Mind if I help?"

Steve asked, "Sure you're up to it?"

Wiley swooped Henry up and into his arms. "Absolutely."

Macy hadn't expected an answer to her rhetorical question, but as tears stung her eyes at the sight of all three of the guys in her life getting along, she realized that yes, life could get sweeter, and she was loving it.

"Did you tell them about the party?" Macy's dad asked her mom.

"Not yet. I was waiting till you were here with me, and it's not just a party, but a reception."

"Oh, well excuse me." Steve snorted and shook his head. "The *queen* and I have decided to throw you two a wedding reception."

"I want to make it big." Adrianne put down her scissors to spread her arms wide. "I want a cake and flowers and balloons. I'm thinking a Western theme, but if you two have something else in mind, I'm happy to discuss options."

"Mom, Dad, thank you, but that's not necessary."

"Yeah," Wiley piped in. "We're good."

Adrianne waved off both of their protests. "I think it's necessary."

"And remember, she's the *queen*." Steve winked, only to have Adrianne chase him out from behind the dining room table to give his backside a swat.

"Don't you listen to a word your father says." Adrianne held out her arms for Wiley to pass her the baby. "My little angel deserves the best, and if your father can build Henry a castle fort, then I can show him off at a fancy party—oh, and this will be a black tie event."

"Mom! Stop. No one around here even has those kinds of clothes. The last time I wore a fancy dress was—" It had been for her wedding with Rex. Not an event she cared to revisit, now that she actually had the makings of her fairy-tale second-chance marriage. "Well, how about we skip the black tie, and just keep it to church suits and dresses?"

Her mom pouted. "I really wanted to see Henry in a tux. My friend Shirley had formal pictures with her grandson, and she already has the most darling scrapbook made of—"

"Wait, so you don't want this party for me and Wiley, but so you can out-scrapbook your friend?"

Steve roared with laughter.

Wiley tried holding back a smile.

Macy already wanted the event over before planning had even started.

"I'M FLATTERED YOUR MOM wants to go to so much effort. It'll probably be fun." After helping Steve with the fort for three hours, they'd packed up Henry and traveled home to the mountain.

"I know, but it seems like an awful lot of fuss."

"Are you really trying to say you don't trust me to keep my shit together at another party?" Wiley was more than ready for his next dose of medicine, and while Macy finished making ham sandwiches at his kitchen counter, he supervised Henry and Blinkie's reunion. Doc had met them at the cabin, and brought not only the dog, but another horse.

"Not at all. Maybe I just don't want to share you."

"Whatever." Since she had her back turned to him, Wiley fished two pills from his bottle, then swallowed them with the last of the warm Dr. Pepper he'd bought at the drug store. "Did I tell you I've got a doctor's appointment in the morning?"

"No. With Dr. Kendrick here in town?" She took pickles from the fridge.

"It's with a guy in Newflower."

"Why so far away?"

He tried stooping to pick up Henry, but a spasm shot through him. Wiley tried to straighten, but a cold sweat accompanied pain so vivid he could only fall back into what had been his grandfather's favorite chair.

"Wiley?"

"Yeah…" He grit his teeth. "I'm good."

She thankfully stayed in the kitchen. "Why didn't you make an appointment here in town?"

"I don't want anyone else in my business, okay?"

Apparently, that was the wrong answer.

Wiley cringed when she banged something metallic against the counter, then appeared before him with her hands on her hips. "FYI—I'm your wife, not just *anyone*. I want to go with you to your appointment."

"No."

*"Yes."*

"Absolutely not. I'm a big boy, and perfectly capable of getting to a doctor on my own."

"This isn't even up for debate. I'm going. End of story."

Wiley was on the verge of escalating the argument, but when Henry started to cry at the raised voices, he changed tactics. "How about if we compromise by you driving me?"

"I want to hear what the doctor says."

"I'll tell you. But I'm a little old to have my hand held at a doctor's appointment. It's embarrassing."

She looked away, but not before he caught her swiping tears from her cheeks. The fact that he'd caused her even a moment's pain was too much, but hell, a man needed his privacy.

"I'm sorry." Even though the drug hadn't yet kicked in, with effort, he stood. "You and Henry tag along. We'll make a fun day of it. Have a nice lunch. Do some shopping. It's going to be great."

"Wiley, the articles I read about PTSD were heartbreaking. Promise, you'll talk to the doctor about what happened during the fireworks."

"I will." He hugged her, and kissed the crown of her head, trying to show her with his body what his words apparently didn't adequately convey—that from now on, he would never hurt her.

"And no more talk of annulments. We're in this together."

"I get it," he said with a nod. "Trust me, okay? I'm fine. You have nothing to worry about other than whether or not the goats are going to screw up your garden as much as they have mine."

IN THE DOCTOR'S waiting room the next morning, Macy tried keeping her focus on the book she was reading to Henry, but it was hard when her every instinct felt she should be with her husband.

So much about his behavior didn't add up.

Before they were married, at times, he'd been cranky and impossible to deal with, but now he had the same dark flashes, but seemed to rein them in. Maybe that was a good sign? And what if she was overthinking everything? Maybe he really was okay, and because of what Rex had put her through, she was assuming every man lied?

"Sweetie," she whispered to Henry, "do you think Mommy's making too big a deal out of your new daddy's meltdown?"

*"Gaaaah!"* Since the baby-speak had been delivered with a smile, she'd take that as a yes.

For such a long time with Rex, her marriage had been a nightmare. The secretive phone calls and late night meetings had been disastrous to her confidence and sense of self-worth. But that was all in the past. Now, she and Wiley had a good thing going.

Why did her heart refuse to believe it?

WILEY PERCHED ON the edge of the exam table, wearing a damned dress and sitting on the equivalent of a rough paper diaper. His nice, safe Dr. Jessie had turned out to be a woman—not that he had anything against the fairer sex serving in the medical profession, but when it came to this particular issue, he would have preferred dealing with a man.

"Mr. James, I understand that you'd like a refill on your meds, but please understand my position. The ultimate goal is to get you off the meds. To do that, you need extensive physical therapy. I spoke with your VA doctor before your appointment, and he said he explained that to you—that the pain meds were strictly to be used as a crutch to get you through the worst of physical therapy. And then, taken only occasionally."

"Great. Well, I currently have an occasional need."

She scribbled something in his chart. What was up with first the punk kid at the pharmacy, and now this woman who didn't look old enough to babysit Henry? She wore her long dark hair in a high ponytail more suitable for a cheerleader than medical professional.

He shifted positions, crinkling the paper under his ass. "Am I good to go?"

"Not just yet. I'm going to set you up with a traveling nurse to get you started on your physical therapy routine. Let's see how you do with outpatient care, but with your level of pain, I'm afraid you may need more aggressive treatment."

"I'm good. Just give me the prescription, and I'll be on my way."

"See?" She tapped her pen against his file. "That desperation leads me to believe you may have a bigger problem than what's going on with your leg. I'm going to be blunt—I'm concerned you're abusing your meds."

"Lord…" He swiped his hand through his too-long hair. "I'm out of here. If you won't give me a prescription, I'll find someone who will—someone who cares about helping a decorated vet lead a normal life."

"I'm sorry you feel that way, Mr. James, but if I didn't care, I would hand over unlimited refills of the drug that I suspect may be doing you more harm than good." She wrote out a limited prescription, gave him a list of VA doctors to contact, told him again about the physical therapy nurse, lectured another ten minutes on the evils of drug addiction, then finally set him free.

The irony in all of this was that he'd never wanted to start taking the meds for fear of ending up addicted, yet now, this doctor who'd only met him once had appointed herself judge and jury by declaring him already in trouble—but he wasn't. Why couldn't anyone see that as long as he had a steady supply of meds, he'd be great?

He wanted so badly to punch the nearest wall, but for the sake of Macy, held his anger in check.

"Hey," she said when he crossed the waiting room to take Henry from her lap. "How'd it go?"

"Perfect. Ready for lunch?"

NEWFLOWER WAS DOUBLE the size of Eagle Ridge, and easily had triple the tourists mingling through the shops on Nugget Avenue—named during the town's fleeting mining fame in the late 1860s. Now the former redbrick bank and assayer's office served as an art gallery and upscale Mexican restaurant, which is where Macy settled Henry into his high chair while waiting for Wiley to return from parking the truck.

She hoped he wouldn't have to walk far.

No matter how much he kept insisting he was fine, she couldn't shake her doubts.

At least fifteen minutes after she'd been seated, he finally joined her. His whole demeanor had changed. After the doctor, he'd been withdrawn and quiet. Now, he treated her to his most irresistible sexy-slow grin. "Sorry that took so long. I found a good spot, but a friend called, and since we hadn't caught up in a while, I lost track of time."

"That's okay. Henry and I have been getting intimately acquainted with the chips and queso. Too bad for you they're almost gone."

He surveyed the empty bowl. "Didn't you vow to obey me and leave me at least a drop of queso?"

"Funny…" Wrinkling her nose, she said, "I don't remember that part of the ceremony."

He leaned to her side of the booth for a kiss. "Doesn't surprise me. You were no doubt in a temporary stupor due to my many charms."

"You are some piece of work."

He stole another kiss. And nothing else mattered but maintaining this magic. Wiley had always been a fixture in her life, but now he was her life. He and Henry meant everything.

From this moment on, she vowed to trust her husband, and to believe he would never do anything to hurt her fragile heart.

## Chapter Seventeen

Life was good.

It was mid-August and since hooking up with a friend of a friend of a friend, Wiley now had a limitless supply of medicine, delivered right to his home. He'd canceled the physical therapy nurse and never returned to that quack doctor.

Because seriously, who knew his body better than he?

He wouldn't say his current uphill hike to the best huckleberries was exactly fun, but with three pills in his system, he could more than handle the climb, or anything else his land required of him. All the animals had been moved to Macy's—even the cat, who now lived on the new front porch. Pancake had taken to lounging in the sun, while her rowdy pups played around her. Just as Doc predicted, the goats and horses and Charlie and his girls had become constant companions.

The junk pile at his grandpa's cabin had been hauled off, and all the fences walked and mended. Plans were in motion for his trail-riding business, and with luck, he'd be open for business in a couple weeks. He now needed medicine every couple hours to keep him working at this peak level, but that was okay. Now that he knew he had plenty, he failed to see a problem in taking it the way his first prescription ordered: *as needed.*

"Are you all right?" Macy asked from behind him. She was out of breath and huffing, but even carrying Henry on his back, Wiley felt fantastic.

"I'm great! Could go all day." He would have walked backward to showboat, but didn't want to risk hurting Henry. "Need a break?"

"Yes. I'm dying." She drank from the bottled water she'd stashed in the berry basket. "I didn't expect it to be this hot."

"If you want to take off your shirt, I'll lose mine."

He loved the sound of her laugh. "Oh, you'd like that, wouldn't you?"

"Henry…" Wiley walked down the trail to his wife. "Hide your eyes, bud. Daddy's got some kissing to do."

Lord, he loved holding Macy against him.

Her curves fit just right, as if they'd been made to be together. Kissing her made him crave more, but a cloud had passed over the sun, and there was a chance of rain for later in the afternoon. He wanted his family safe back in the cabin by then.

"Mmm…" Macy held her eyes closed when they paused for air. "Not that I care to make your ego any bigger, but, Wiley James, you sure do know how to make a girl happy."

"Thank you, ma'am." He tipped his straw hat to her. "But if you want enough berries to make jam, we need to get going."

"Agreed. I'm not liking the look of this sky."

In another thirty minutes, the clouds had cleared, and they reached the sunny glade where their families had been picking huckleberries for almost a hundred years. Wiley's great-grandfather had been a miner, and when that failed, he'd turned to trapping to earn a living. It had been a rough life, but according to Buster's recollections, satisfying.

Once Macy spread a quilt for Henry to lounge on, then

slathered him in a fresh layer of sunscreen, she joined Wiley in picking.

He asked, "Remember the time we came up here with your grandma and found a bear cleaning every bush?"

"Sure do. I also remember Grandma aiming her shotgun straight for his behind."

"She was a damned good shot." Wiley plucked five fat berries to add to their growing pile. "Used to put both our grandfathers to shame."

"Yes, she did."

He moved on to the next bush. "Think there's any way we could get her to your mom's party?"

"I suppose we could try. It all depends on how she's doing. When we went to see her right after the wedding, she didn't recognize either of us, so it might not be a good idea to take her to an unfamiliar place."

"Guess you're right." Clouds had moved back over the sun. Since they'd married, Wiley regularly visited Dot with Macy. The afternoons were hard on her. Dot didn't recognize either of them, and inevitably upon leaving, Macy cried. His heart ached for her. "I miss them—our grandparents. If it weren't for them, we might not be together."

"True." She moved to the bush beside him. "But then like you used to tell me, maybe I would have been better off? Not hitching myself to a no-good cowboy."

"Who are you calling no good?" He lunged to tackle her.

"You!" Just before he reached her, she took off running.

They crisscrossed the meadow until Wiley's leg pain got the best of him. In order to avoid showing weakness, he tackled her to the soft grass, then plucked a pretty yellow wildflower and tucked it behind her ear.

"You need to take that back." He tickled her ribs and belly.

"No way!" She laughed through tears. "Stop! I'm gonna pee!"

"Good for you we brought extra diapers." He tickled her all the harder, and the more she laughed, the more Henry laughed, too.

The baby was a strong crawler, and he decided to join in on the fun.

Wiley tickled him, too.

Winded, Wiley sat back. "Good thing we left Blinkie at home, or he'd be yapping up a storm."

"Probably." She pointed to the sky. "Speaking of which, we should get going. Those clouds are looking darker."

As if on cue, thunder rolled.

"Don't have to ask me twice." He offered Macy his hand to help her to her feet.

While she got Henry settled in his backpack carrier, Wiley combined the contents of their baskets. He shook Henry's quilt, then folded it to stash in a zipper compartment of the infant's ride.

His leg was starting to hurt. He reached for his medicine, only to find his pill bottle no longer in his pocket. He had more at the house, but the return hike was treacherous—not something he was capable of stone sober.

Returning to the berry bushes, he kicked at the tall grasses, hoping it would be on the surface. No such luck.

"Drop something?" Macy asked.

"My medicine." He searched the area where they'd roughhoused.

"You've got more at the house, don't you? Since you started the mail-order prescription service, seems like they send way more than you need."

"I know, right?"

"Well, even though you're not due for your next dose for a couple hours, that's one more reason for us to get home. Want me to take Henry and you carry the baskets?"

*No. Hell, no.* But what if his knee gave out on the trail? It wouldn't. He refused to let it.

"Wiley? There's no shame in needing help, you know?"

"I don't need help. Let's just go."

The playful vibe had been squashed—at least in his mind.

Lightning cracked and the resulting thunder crashed far too close for comfort. His heart raced.

*Incoming! Get those kids out of there!*

He pressed his fingertips to his forehead, willing his mind to focus on the task at hand.

Macy helped settle Henry on Wiley's back.

Wiley fastened the waistband support, then gestured for Macy to lead the way. "Ladies first."

"I'd rather stay behind to keep an eye on the baby."

Lightning cracked again. Thunder shook the ground.

For a split second, Wiley closed his eyes and saw his pal Crow. *"Go! I'm already gone."*

*There was blood, so much blood. Crow's legs had been sliced off by a car windshield and he sat in a pool of gushing red. But it wasn't just his blood.*

*Schoolkids were in pieces.*

*His brain couldn't fully process the carnage.*

*A backpack here. A severed hand there.*

*He tried staying strong, but retched. He pulled himself together, knowing he had to save Crow.*

*Another bomb hit, and another—maybe gunfire. His ears had stopped working, and the once blue sky had turned an inky, billowy black. Wiley dragged his dead friend as far as his own injuries allowed, but then he fell.*

*The bombs kept coming.*

*The earth kept shaking.*

*He covered his ears with his hands. Would the noise ever stop?*

"Wiley? Talk to me? What's wrong? The lightning's bad. We have to go."

Lightning. Thunder.

Reality rushed back, along with a fierce wind gust. He was no longer in Syria, but home. On the mountain where only good resided.

"Wiley, please." Macy tugged his arm. "Move. What's wrong with you?"

"Nothing. Let's go." He stumbled into action. He couldn't save Crow, but Macy and Henry were his new charges. He would see them to safety or die trying.

BACK AT THE CABIN, while rain hammered the tin roof, Macy gave Henry a warm bath and bottle to help calm him after he'd panicked from the shock of the storm, then dressed him in cozy pj's, and settled him in his crib for a nap.

She should have kept him awake till bedtime, but the little guy could hardly keep his eyes open.

Next, Macy focused on her own comfort, filling the tub to the brim with steaming water.

Sinking up to her neck, she released the breath she felt as if she'd been holding since the first thunderclap.

"Hey…" Wiley carried a steaming mug of cocoa, and set it on the windowsill behind the tub. "You always used to like hot chocolate during a storm."

"Don't."

"What? I just brought you a warm drink, not a martini."

"Wiley, the lightning and thunder brought on another of your PTSD spells. Don't even try denying it. No matter how hard I shook you, you were *gone*. Do you have any idea how terrifying that was for me?"

"I'm sorry. It won't happen again."

"How can you say that? Sure, you can avoid fireworks,

or I don't know, a gun range, but you can't control the weather. I needed you up there, but you'd checked out."

"I said I'm sorry. I'm not Superman, okay?"

"I don't want you to be. All I'm asking is for you to be man enough to realize you need help and not be too prideful to ask for it. When we got married, we became a team, but you act like a solo player."

"The hell I do. I'll admit, at first, I wasn't fully on board with this whole marriage thing." He lowered himself to sit on the closed toilet. His mask of concentration told her he was in pain. "But lately, everything I am is centered around you and Henry. All I want is the best for you."

"Then go back to the doctor. Start physical therapy. Find a shrink to get help with your blackout spells."

"No. I'm fine. Granted, I was preoccupied by the storm, but we all got down in one piece, didn't we?" He pushed himself up, only to kneel beside her. Dipping his hand beneath the water, he pressed his open palm to her chest. Could he feel her racing pulse? "You mean everything to me. I would never do anything that could hurt you or Henry. Trust me."

"I want to…" She took his dear hand, pressing it to her cheek. "Wiley, you mean the world to me, but what you're going through—it's bigger than I thought. Maybe Dad was right? Maybe you were right? Is whatever's happening with you too much for me to fix?" Her throat ached from the effort of holding back tears.

"Why are you bringing that up when everything's been so right?"

"Because honestly? I'm scared of losing you." That very real possibility played a game of Russian roulette with her heart.

WILEY WASN'T PROUD of the fact, but he'd lost count of how many painkillers he took a day to be the man Macy needed him to be. Three weeks had passed since the storm that had come unacceptably close to tearing them apart. He hadn't had another spell since then, and didn't plan on ever having another.

Life had been hectic, but good.

As soon as he got more horses, his trail-riding business would soon open.

They'd made huckleberry jam and found good homes for three of Pancake's five puppies. Doc had brought over a new half-starved mare and Charlie and his crew were still undecided about whether or not to accept her. So far, signs were positive, and she'd already put on a few pounds. Lulu and the goats had gained a little too much.

Henry was pulling himself up regularly, and Macy had gone nuts safety-proofing the cabin. The cat—Popcorn, Macy's name choice, not his—had taken to sitting atop Macy's grandmother's upright piano and didn't seem amused by the commotion.

Tonight was the reception Adrianne was holding, and Wiley hoped this was also the night Macy finally admitted everything was going great.

"What can I do to help?" Wiley asked Macy, who did her makeup at her grandmother's vanity table.

"Could you please check Henry's diaper bag. I think I used the last can of formula, and he needs spare pj's since Mom and Dad said they want to keep him for the night."

"I like the sound of that." She wore her hair up, and he kissed her neck. "I'm down for adult fun after the party."

"Me, too." She smiled at him in the mirror, and he smiled back.

"You look beautiful. I like that dress." Her mom had taken her and Wendy for a ladies' weekend in Missoula and come back with a shiny blue number that made her eyes sparkle.

"Thank you. I like your suit." Before now, the closest he'd come to wearing a suit had been his dress whites when he'd been on active duty, but he'd always been so proud to don the uniform, he'd viewed it as more of a privilege than duty.

There was so much more he wanted—needed—to say.

He wanted to apologize for the lackluster way he'd entered their marriage and to reassure her he was now in this for the long haul. His medicine supply would last forever, which meant she never had to worry about another of his spells.

"Okay, well…" He hitched his thumb toward the kitchen. "I'll get started on packing Henry's gear."

"Wiley?"

"Yeah?" His pulse raced at the softness of her somber tone.

"I, well…" She licked her full lips, and then they curved up at the corners. He'd seen a lot of amazing things during his time in the Navy, but never had he seen any sight more spellbinding than her current smile. "Let's have an amazing night."

"The best." He exhaled. "It's gonna be great."

"Yes, it is." She blew him a kiss.

His stupid-fast pulse craved the real deal, but since she'd already put on lipstick, he blew a kiss back, counting his lucky stars.

"Aw, LOOK AT YOU." Macy's mom had allowed the grown-ups to wear semiformal, but she'd insisted on Henry wearing a minitux. "You're the perfect gentleman. When my scrapbooking club sees you, they're all going to turn clover-green with envy."

"Geez, Mom," Macy teasingly complained. "How about Wiley and me? Didn't we polish up nice, too?"

"Oh, of course. Stand together so I can take in the full picture."

"You don't have your camera," Wiley pointed out.

"Oh—I have a photographer coming. For now, I want to plan the perfect scenes."

Macy turned to Wiley and shook her head. "Sorry. I should have warned you before we tied the knot just what a loony bin you were marrying into."

He laughed while hugging her mom.

The happy sight had tears welling in Macy's eyes. She'd been tense ever since the storm, but now released that tension in favor of enjoying this carefree Wiley. Over the past few weeks, he'd worked wonders with the cabin. The place hadn't looked so good since her grandfather had been alive. Henry was always grinning, and even sourpuss Charlie seemed to have lightened his demeanor. All was so right in her world that she refused to anticipate any more problems.

The calm, sixty-degree night was a little on the nippy side, but after a rowdy line dance, the cool air felt good.

Her parents had gone all out—hiring a local country band, ordering a gorgeous four-tiered cake, and even stringing thousands of fairy lights in their backyard trees. While the big folks danced and talked and ate fancy snacks like steak-on-a-stick and gourmet mini-corn dogs, the little folks had a ball playing in Henry's new fort.

Poor Henry had conked out in his playpen, and everyone in the family took turns checking on him.

Wiley seemed in his element, and all the females from high school girls to the white-haired crowd were smitten. Macy took great pride in knowing he was all hers.

"Wanna dance?" he asked into her ear. His warm breath tickled and made her shiver.

"Depends on if I can wrangle you from your fan club."

He rolled his eyes, then kissed her dizzy in front of

God, her parents and practically the whole town. "In case you haven't gotten the memo, you're the only one I want."

"Good." Happy, she stood on her tiptoes to kiss him right back.

The night moseyed along in a happy blur. They cut the cake, and fed each other bites. They shared a champagne toast, after which Macy shared a dance with her father.

"I owe you an apology," he said, swaying her in time to the slow, sweet tune.

"What for?"

"When you first told me Wiley was back on the mountain, I'd heard enough about him to make me scared, but turns out, he's grown into a fine young man. I couldn't be prouder for you to be with him."

"Thank you, Dad. Your approval means the world to me."

"Well, you've got it and then some. Your mom and I have really grown to love him, and it's no secret you and Henry do, too."

Since her throat was too tight from emotion to speak, Macy nodded. She finally composed herself enough to manage saying, "I do. I really do."

"All right, enough of this sappy stuff." Her dad wiped tears from his eyes. "Your mom and I have one last surprise for you two that we hope will be fun. Took some doing, but I think it will put the perfect cap on what has already been a pretty great night."

"You know I can't stand surprises. What is it?"

"Can't tell you. Your momma would have my hide."

"You're terrible." But she loved him. In fact, her heart was so full of love for her parents and husband and child, and all of their wonderful friends that once the dance was over, she dashed to her childhood bedroom's bathroom to compose herself.

It didn't take long to freshen her makeup and smooth her hair. When she finished, she and Wendy spent a good fifteen minutes gossiping on Macy's twin bed about a new guy Wendy had met.

Macy was headed back outside when she heard some odd popping sounds, then crackling, followed by full-on explosions.

Pulse quickening, she ran to the backyard to find a full-scale fireworks show already underway.

"Surprise!" her parents said in unison. Then her mom added, "Your dad pulled a few strings with the fire marshal to allow us to put on a show. Aren't they gorgeous? Since you two were too busy messing around on the Fourth of July, we thought you might enjoy another show that you actually get to watch."

Macy had no words.

Wiley. She had to find him.

"Macy?" her mom asked. "Where are you going? Stay and watch the show."

"I have to find Wiley."

"Relax," her dad said. "I want you to catch every last pop. Last I saw him, Wiley was shooting the breeze with some of your old high school friends."

Despite her parents' misgivings, Macy looked everywhere, only to find Wiley was gone. Even worse—she feared he'd taken Henry with him.

## Chapter Eighteen

Enemy fire rained fast and hard.

Wiley tucked the baby against his chest and ran until his lungs burned. At all costs, his number-one mission directive was to save this child. He would never let another child die on his watch.

Deeper and deeper into dense woods he ran until finding suitable temporary shelter beneath a rock overhang. He must have dropped his radio during the cross fire as it wasn't on him—neither was his piece. He never took a piss without his SIG SAUER P226, but he'd checked all his pockets, and it was gone.

Okay, he'd been in worse jams.

Judging by the light and sound, the enemy was a good two or three klicks away. He'd assess the status of his civilian, then reassess. In his book, the more distance between him and the rebels, the better.

"How are you doing, little buddy?" He held out the infant child. He'd been crying, but now slept. Poor guy was no doubt exhausted. "If you don't mind, we're gonna press deeper, then I'll devise a way for us to meet back with my team. Crow's gotta be close. I know he was right on my tail."

The deeper into the night Wiley trudged, the more confused he grew. His left leg hurt like a son of a bitch. Had he been shot or taken shrapnel?

He pressed on until he could physically go no farther.

The moonless night closed in.

He'd give his left nut for his night-vision goggles and his right for a standard-issue flashlight.

He settled into another overhang.

The air was cold, so he removed his jacket, wrapping it around the infant for extra warmth.

He'd have felt a lot better with a fire, but with the enemy close, it was too risky. He dug a shallow hollow then placed the infant in it for added insulation from the night air. Wiley used his pocketknife to hack off a few low-hanging conifer branches that he then used to cover them both. The greenery would serve dual purposes—camouflage and protection from the elements.

It was hardly a nice, comfy tent on the outskirts of Baghdad, but it would do.

He probably needed shut-eye, but couldn't risk the infant's well-being, so he held his knife, ready for possible close combat at a moment's call.

"WHAT DO YOU MEAN he's afraid of fireworks?" Adrianne asked when Macy told her she suspected Wiley wasn't himself and had taken Henry with him. "Wiley's a big, tough guy. I didn't know he was afraid of anything."

"Mom, please stay out of it. Dad, I've done some reading and I'm hardly an expert, but I think Wiley suffers from pretty bad PTSD. He tries hiding it, but with each episode, it's steadily grown worse." She gave her father the short version of all the other times Wiley had been in trouble, and soon enough, her dad agreed with her possible diagnosis.

Steve approached the band's mic. "Sorry, everyone, but

as you may have guessed, we've got a bit of a situation." He explained the gist of what had happened, then asked, "If all of you would please find a flashlight, let's meet back here in ten minutes, then split off into groups to find Wiley and my grandson. They can't have gotten too far."

Macy hoped her father was right in that they'd find Wiley and Henry close and unharmed. She couldn't imagine what her son must be going through, and after this shocking escalation to Wiley's obviously unstable mental condition, she worried about him, too.

Hugging herself, she questioned her every move since her reunion with him. How could she have been so naive? So blinded by his good looks and charm that she hadn't insisted he see a therapist back on the Fourth of July?

"How are you holding up?" Wendy asked, flashlight in hand.

"How do you think? If anything happens to Henry, it'll be all my fault."

"I'm sure Henry is fine," Wendy said with another hug. "Wiley's a good guy. He just needs help—which we'll all do our best to help him find."

Macy wished she could be so sure.

An hour passed with no sign of her husband or son.

Two hours melded into three as the search widened from the neighborhood to the surrounding area, and then finally, the dark menacing forest where Macy was terrified to go.

She wanted to help with the search, but her father refused her offer, thinking it best she stay home safe with her mom, making sandwiches and coffee for the hundred-plus volunteers who had switched from party to rescue mode.

The sun had just risen when a police deputy's radio squawked. Her father's party had picked up Wiley's trail and they now heard a baby crying. He requested that Macy ride out on a four-wheeler with warm clothes, a bottle and a diaper.

"He's o-okay," Macy managed on the heels of a sob. "Henry has to be okay."

"What about Wiley?" Adrianne asked the deputy. "Ask my husband if he knows anything more."

"Mom, I'm afraid to know. What if Wiley's so far gone he can't come back?"

"If that's the case, we'll handle it one day—one minute—at a time. For now, all we know is that he needs help. Go to him. Help him heal."

Macy choked back fresh tears and nodded.

MACY WISHED SHE could have been angry. It was so much easier to bear than the sorrow gripping her chest upon finding Wiley, cradling her son. He sat crouched under a rock overhang, staring blankly ahead while holding an open pocketknife.

She climbed off the four-wheeler a deputy had driven, then approached her dad. "What can I do?"

"Slowly go to him. Play along with whatever scenario he's stuck in. I've got calls out to a couple friends who have lived through this and come out okay. He's a good man, Macy. Yes, he's done a horrible, horrible thing by running off with the baby, but I suspect he only wanted to save Henry from perceived danger—never to harm him."

Macy sniffed back tears, then squared her shoulders.

Each step seemed to take a lifetime.

Her father had coached her to make no sudden moves. Behind her, a half-dozen men stood by with firearms should her conversation with Wiley take an unexpected turn. Macy prayed it didn't come to that.

"Wiley?" About ten feet away, she stopped. "Can you hear me? It's Macy. I'm here to help."

He straightened, then saluted. "Master Chief Wiley James, reporting for duty. Are you here to provide the civilian and myself safe transport back to my team?"

"Y-yes." Macy's heart shattered.

Henry was fine, nestled safe and snug in Wiley's capable arms, tugging at his nose. His cheeks were dirt-smudged and hair a mess, but of course, Wiley hadn't hurt him. How could he when he was hurt himself?

"Do you have a radio? I need to report my status to my team. The civilian infant is unharmed, and there has been no sign of enemy fire since dawn."

Where had he gone? Where was the strong, capable, charming cowboy she'd so desperately loved that she'd ignored every warning ringing in her soul? She no longer blamed Wiley for any of this, but herself. He'd told her all along he wasn't ready for marriage, and he'd been right.

"Ma'am? Your radio?"

"Sure. I've got one." She wiped silent, messy tears with the backs of her hands. "If you'll follow me, I'll take you to it."

"Great."

"Would you mind if I hold the infant?"

"Ma'am, I'm not sure that's a good idea. I've been charged with his safekeeping."

She choked back fresh tears. "I understand. Follow me, and everything's going to be okay." Only it wouldn't. Even love wasn't strong enough to fix this mess. Wiley might be lost to her and there wasn't a damned thing she could do to fix him. Or the hole in her heart.

WILEY HAD NO IDEA how much time had passed when he came to. The last thing he remembered was dancing with Macy at their party, then he woke here—in an unremarkable hospital room with his arms and legs restrained.

Pain shot through his leg, radiating into his back.

His mouth was dry and stomach queasy.

"You're awake."

Wiley glanced toward the curtain-covered window to find Macy's dad. "What happened? How long have I been out?"

"A few days. You've been in and out while coming down from your meds. You're in a Missoula hospital psych ward. Adrianne and I had the bright idea to end your party with a bang by hosting a fireworks show, then—"

Wiley groaned. "I don't want to know what comes next."

"No one saw you leave, but you snatched up Henry, and ran off with him into the woods. We found you bivouacked the next morning beneath a rock overhang. You did a good job of protecting him against what your mind perceived as a grave threat. Only there was no danger. Which is why we're going to get you some help."

"Not that I deserve to speak with her, but where's Macy?"

"She went to grab a bite to eat with her mom. They should be back soon."

"Think you could get me out of these?"

Steve obliged. "Don't even think about bolting."

"Trust me," he released a sad chuckle, "as bad as my leg hurts, I couldn't go anywhere if I tried." He pressed the heels of his hands to his forehead. "I'm sorry. I thought I had everything under control, but—"

The door creaked open, then Adrianne and Macy walked through.

"You're up." Adrianne approached him for a hug.

He wanted Macy, to touch her, talk to her, try to make sense out of this nightmare he didn't begin to understand.

Steve cleared his throat. "Adrianne, how about you take me to get some coffee."

"But, I— Oh, yes. Let's go. Macy, hon, I've got my cell if you need us."

"Thanks, Mom." She leaned against the wall farthest from Wiley's bed.

When his in-laws had left, Wiley said, "I'm sorry. I don't even remember what I've done, but you have to know I'm—"

Macy stormed across the floor to throw her arms around him, her body racked with sobs. She didn't stop crying until the chest of his hospital gown was soaked with her tears. "I h-hate you."

"I don't blame you."

"You lied—so many times. About *everything*. And then you had another spell and ran off with Henry. I was so scared—terrified—one or both of you might have been hurt."

"I'm sorry. I'm fine."

"Don't you dare tell me you're fine, Wiley James, because you're not. God knows how many pain pills you've been taking and lying the whole time. I'm not stupid. I finally put two and two together and realized it's not normal for pain meds to arrive in a bucket."

"I'm sorry."

"You played me for a fool—and my family and all of our friends. And for what? Your pride? At any time, you could have come to any of us for help, but you were too damned stubborn. You knew my ex broke my heart, and when I begged you time and again to be straight with me about how bad you were hurting, and about how many meds you were taking, and about your PTSD, you lied. You're a horrible, despicable man, and I hate you. I *hate* you."

"I love you."

*"Why can't I stop loving you?"* Her tears started again.

She leaned over to press her cheek to his chest, all the while fisting his gown.

"You should hate me." He stroked her impossibly soft red curls. "I hate myself for hurting you. If this is the part where you tell me you're leaving me, I won't stop you. I don't deserve you—never did—and if it's what you want, I'll let you go."

"No, Wiley, you won't. I wish leaving you would be that easy, but how can I ever be truly rid of you when you've always been in my heart?"

Hope he didn't deserve, but so badly wanted, swelled inside him. "So what do you want to do?"

"Mom's going to watch Henry while Dad and I drive you to Texas. Dad found an inpatient clinic that specializes in treating PTSD and drug addiction, and will also get you the physical therapy you need for your leg to no longer be in constant pain. They don't know how long it will take to make you whole, but when they do, Henry and I will be up on the mountain, waiting for you to come home."

# Epilogue

*Six months later*

"Charlie, if you don't get your stubborn behind out of the garden, I'm going to spank you with this hoe."

He spit, but luckily trotted back toward the pasture to where the relatively well-behaved goats and horses grazed. Doc had brought six more horses to be rehabilitated, and just as Wiley had planned, Macy, with the help of a couple good ex-rodeo cowboys Doc highly recommended, started his small-scale trail-riding stable for tourists, although now that winter had set in, business was slow.

It seemed as if it had been forever since Wiley had been home, but today was the day he'd return. She wasn't sure how to feel. Part giddy. Part apprehensive. Part panic-stricken.

She wasn't sure what to do or say.

She and Henry had visited him for Thanksgiving and Christmas.

They talked on the phone as often as Wiley was allowed, but mostly, they'd exchanged letters. Deep, thought-provoking letters about everything from how much they loved each other to their plans for the future to how Wiley felt about getting released.

He'd admitted to being scared. Humbled.

His memories of what happened with Henry had eventually returned, and he'd been sickened by his behavior. But since Macy and her family had forgiven him, she'd urged him to forgive himself.

At the foot of the porch stairs, Pancake lounged in the unseasonably warm sun. Her two pups were nearly as big as she, and loved nothing more than baying at Popcorn who never much budged from the porch or piano.

Blinkie and Henry had become inseparable, but now that the toddler was walking, the dog had learned to run faster to keep up.

Hands on her hips, Macy surveyed the cabin and grounds, wishing for an early spring. Snow covered most everything, but patches of grass at least provided hope that warmer days were to come.

The task of prepping the garden for an early planting wasn't especially fun, but it kept her mind off Wiley. She felt more like a teen about to embark on her first date than a married woman with a child.

She worked until Henry tripped and got snow in his mouth, then took him inside to wash up.

She baked oatmeal cookies so the house would smell like a home.

So she didn't have to cook when she'd rather be visiting, she made a meat loaf and mashed potatoes and green beans for dinner.

By six, darkness was settling around the cabin, and Macy feared losing a good bit of her mind from anticipation.

But then her father's truck's headlights shone through the front window, and she swooped up Henry and ran for the door.

Her dad beat Wiley from the truck. "You two are a sight for sore eyes. Man, that's a long stretch of highway."

Wiley emerged. He'd shaved, wore his hair in a buzz cut, and walked with what looked to be a hand-carved cane. In his usual stubble's absence, faint scars were now visible on his cheek and chin.

For the longest time, Macy stood in the dying sun, staring at her husband as if he was a mirage. How many nights had she lain awake, dreaming of this moment? Yet now that it was here, her limbs had turned gangly and awkward and unsure.

"Hey," Wiley said.

"Hey, yourself, cowboy."

He held his battered straw hat in hand, and when she met him at the bottom of the steps, he put it on Henry's head. Then he happened to glance down at her swollen belly and tears sprang to his eyes.

"Surprise…" She stood on her tiptoes to kiss him, shyly laughing when their baby got in the way.

He hung his cane on the porch rail to brace both hands on the miracle growing inside her. "How did you keep this from me? All those letters. Why didn't you ever…" He shook his head. "Doesn't matter."

"I wanted you to worry about you. If you'd known I was carrying our baby girl, I'm afraid you would have gone and done something stupid like checking yourself out of the facility."

"Probably true," he said with a wry nod. "And you—" He grinned and pointed to Steve. "Some kind of friend you turned out to be, keeping this big a secret."

"It wasn't easy, but I had selfish motives for wanting you to get back to Eagle Ridge just as fast as you safely could."

"Oh, yeah? Why's that?"

Macy's heart galloped when Wiley put his arm around her shoulders, drawing her close.

"Because I'm damn sick and tired of helping your wife care for all of these doggone animals Doc Carthage keeps bringing."

As if on cue, Blinkie and Pancake barked.

Charlie and his angels and the goats and horses stood at the fence rail, watching the proceedings as if they'd also awaited Wiley's return.

Henry wriggled to be let down to chase the dogs, so Macy set him to his feet.

"Look at him go." Wiley teared up all over again. "I've missed so much."

"Yeah, but look how much you now have to look forward to."

He pulled her into a lingering kiss, during which her dad cleared his throat.

"If y'all don't mind," Steve said with a big wink, "I'm gonna go smooch on my wife."

"Bye, Dad." Macy crushed him in a hug. "Thank you for everything you've done."

Wiley repeated the sentiment.

"It's been my pleasure," he said on his way to the truck. "But Wiley, from now on, I'll expect to see you nice and regular down at the VFW. It's high time the boys and I had new blood for Tuesday night poker."

"Yessir, I'll be there."

Arm in arm, Macy stood with Wiley, waving while her dad drove off.

"Now, what do you want to do?" Wiley asked.

"Anything you want—except for ever leaving me again."

\* \* \* \* \*

# REQUEST YOUR FREE BOOKS!
## 2 FREE NOVELS PLUS 2 FREE GIFTS!

◆ HARLEQUIN®

# ᴀ American Romance®

## LOVE, HOME & HAPPINESS

**YES!** Please send me 2 FREE Harlequin® American Romance® novels and my 2 FREE gifts (gifts are worth about $10). After receiving them, if I don't wish to receive any more books, I can return the shipping statement marked "cancel." If I don't cancel, I will receive 4 brand-new novels every month and be billed just $4.74 per book in the U.S. or $5.49 per book in Canada. That's a savings of at least 12% off the cover price! It's quite a bargain! Shipping and handling is just 50¢ per book in the U.S. and 75¢ per book in Canada.* I understand that accepting the 2 free books and gifts places me under no obligation to buy anything. I can always return a shipment and cancel at any time. Even if I never buy another book, the two free books and gifts are mine to keep forever.

154/354 HDN GHZZ

Name _____ (PLEASE PRINT) _____

Address _____ Apt. # _____

City _____ State/Prov. _____ Zip/Postal Code _____

Signature (if under 18, a parent or guardian must sign) _____

### Mail to the **Reader Service:**
**IN U.S.A.:** P.O. Box 1867, Buffalo, NY 14240-1867
**IN CANADA:** P.O. Box 609, Fort Erie, Ontario L2A 5X3

**Want to try two free books from another line?**
**Call 1-800-873-8635 or visit www.ReaderService.com.**

* Terms and prices subject to change without notice. Prices do not include applicable taxes. Sales tax applicable in N.Y. Canadian residents will be charged applicable taxes. Offer not valid in Quebec. This offer is limited to one order per household. Not valid for current subscribers to Harlequin American Romance books. All orders subject to credit approval. Credit or debit balances in a customer's account(s) may be offset by any other outstanding balance owed by or to the customer. Please allow 4 to 6 weeks for delivery. Offer available while quantities last.

**Your Privacy**—The Reader Service is committed to protecting your privacy. Our Privacy Policy is available online at www.ReaderService.com or upon request from the Reader Service.

We make a portion of our mailing list available to reputable third parties that offer products we believe may interest you. If you prefer that we not exchange your name with third parties, or if you wish to clarify or modify your communication preferences, please visit us at www.ReaderService.com/consumerchoice or write to us at Reader Service Preference Service, P.O. Box 9062, Buffalo, NY 14240-9062. Include your complete name and address.

HARI5

A soft, concerned and decidedly male voice interrupted her from just outside the corral.

"Are you all right?"

She quickly gathered herself, using the sleeve of her denim jacket to wipe her face. "I'm fine," she said, sounding stronger than she felt.

"You sure?"

She dared a peek over the top of Hurry Up's mane, only to quickly duck down.

Josh Dempsey, August's oldest son, stood watching her. She recognized his brown Resistol cowboy hat and tan canvas duster through the sucker rod railing. Of all the people to find her, why him?

Heat raced up her neck and engulfed her face. Not from embarrassment, but anger. It wasn't that she didn't like Josh. Okay, to be honest, she didn't like him. He'd made it clear from the moment he'd arrived at Dos Estrellas a few months ago that he wanted the land belonging to the mustang sanctuary.

She understood. To a degree. The cattle operation was the sole source of income for the ranch, and the sanctuary—operating mostly on donations—occupied a significant amount of valuable pastureland. In addition,

Cara didn't technically own the land. She'd simply been granted use of the two sections and the right to reside in the ranch house for as long as she wanted or for as long as the ranch remained in the family.

Sympathy for the struggling cattle operation didn't change her feelings. She needed the sanctuary. She and the two-hundred-plus horses that would otherwise be homeless. For those reasons, she refused to concede, causing friction in the family.

Additional friction. Gabe Dempsey and his half brothers, Josh and Cole, were frequently at odds over the ranch, the terms of their late father's will and the mustang sanctuary.

"You need some help?" Josh asked from the other side of the corral.

"No."

"Okay."

But he didn't leave.

Without having to glance up, she felt his height and the breadth of his wide shoulders. He looked at her with those piercing blue eyes of his.

She'd seen his eyes flash with anger—at his brother Gabe and at her for having the audacity to stand up to him. She'd also seen them soften when he talked about his two children.

"I'm sorry," he said with a tenderness in his voice that she'd never heard before. "Violet told me earlier. About your son."

*Don't miss COME HOME, COWBOY by Cathy McDavid,*
*part of the **MUSTANG VALLEY** miniseries,*
*available February 2016 wherever*
*Harlequin® American Romance®*
*books and ebooks are sold.*

www.Harlequin.com

# Love the Harlequin book you just read?

Your opinion matters.

Review this book on your favorite book site, review site, blog or your own social media properties and share your opinion with other readers!

**Be sure to connect with us at:**
Harlequin.com/Newsletters
Facebook.com/HarlequinBooks
Twitter.com/HarlequinBooks

# THE WORLD IS BETTER WITH

*Romance*

Harlequin has everything from contemporary, passionate and heartwarming to suspenseful and inspirational stories.

Whatever your mood, we have a romance just for you!

Connect with us to find your next great read, special offers and more.

**f** /HarlequinBooks

**🐦** @HarlequinBooks

www.HarlequinBlog.com

www.Harlequin.com/Newsletters

**H HARLEQUIN®**

A *Romance* FOR EVERY MOOD™

www.Harlequin.com